CLA RLD
AY 2023 - ISSUE 200

FICTION

Better Living Through Algorithms — *Naomi Kritzer* *1*
Through the Roof of the World — *Harry Turtledove* *14*
To Sail Beyond the Botnet — *Suzanne Palmer* *28*
LOL, Said the Scorpion — *Rich Larson* *80*
Sensation and Sensibility — *Parker Ragland* *88*
The Giants Among Us — *Megan Chee* *95*
Action at a Distance — *An Hao* *102*
The Fall — *Jordan Chase-Young* *114*

NON-FICTION

Horror and Science Fiction: Genre's Evil Twins — *Carrie Sessarego* 121
Gods Aren't Necessarily Nice:
A Conversation with Premee Mohamed — *Arley Sorg* 128
Exploration And Healing:
A Conversation with Megan O'Keefe — *Arley Sorg* 141
Editor's Desk: Something Went Mostly Right — *Neil Clarke* 147
Taking a Sample (Cover Art) — *Arthur Haas* 151

Neil Clarke: Publisher/Editor-in-Chief
Sean Wallace: Editor
Kate Baker: Non-Fiction Editor/Podcast Director

Clarkesworld Magazine (ISSN: 1937-7843) • Issue 200 • May 2023

clarkesworldmagazine.com

Better Living Through Algorithms

NAOMI KRITZER

June was the first of my friends to get into it. This isn't surprising—she was playing Wordle for weeks before Margo or I discovered it. When we met up for our weekly lunch, she kept checking her phone and I assumed it was some new game. Then she put it down with a smile and said, "Abelique told me not to pick up my phone again until after lunch was over."

"Who?" Margo said.

"It's this new app for better living."

"I love the idea of an *app* that tells you to *put your phone down more.* For your own good," Margo said, her eyes glinting.

"You should try it!" June said. "You get the first thirty days free!"

"And after that, you have to pay someone to nag you to use your phone less?"

"It's more than that." June took a bite out of her tuna melt. "For one thing, you also agree to occasionally nag other people to put *their* phones down."

Margo and I both laughed, and June flushed. But she did not, I noticed, touch her phone again until we were ready to leave the diner.

Sometimes, once you hear about a new thing, suddenly it's just *everywhere.*

It was like that with Abelique. I couldn't un-see it. Or un-hear it, really, because it's not like I was peering over people's shoulders at their phones, I was overhearing people talking about it. Abelique told them to make clam chowder for dinner. Abelique had assigned them a movie to watch. Abelique sent them to bed at nine p.m. It was that last one that caught my attention enough that I actually looked it up. "A complete lifestyle app" was what Wikipedia called it. This was not actually all that enlightening.

"I think it's a cult," Margo said the following week as we were waiting for a table.

"You said the same thing about Pokemon Go," I said.

"Okay, but I was *joking* about Pokemon Go," she said. "Abelique really is a cult. People sign up for this thing and then just do whatever it tells them to do."

"It can't *make* you do anything," June said, coming up behind us and overhearing.

"So what did it definitely not make you do in the last day?" Margo asked. "Just give us a rundown, June."

"Last night it had me try a new recipe, which was really good, and then it had me watch a movie I hadn't heard of, which was also really good, and then I got my bedtime phone call—"

"Your *what*."

"I mean, no one's going to go to bed just because an app reminder comes up so there's a phone tree. You get a call, and you make a call."

"You have to use your phone as a *phone?* I'm out," I said.

"Are you considering trying it?" June said, eagerly. "You should!"

"I don't trust anything that's free for thirty days," I said. "Because I know myself. And I will *forget.*"

"You won't forget with Abelique because you'll get a reminder phone call." She turned back to Margo. "Maybe you could try it, and then write about it." Margo had been trying to freelance as a tech journalist, when she wasn't doing marketing writing to pay the bills.

Margo smacked her own forehead, exasperated. "I'm going to give up on freelance journalism. People keep offering me fifty dollars for something that would take a hundred hours of research. Can we talk about something else? Like that movie you watched?"

June told us about the movie—it had come out about ten years ago, and none of us had heard about it at the time, and it sounded pretty good, actually. Margo looked up a review. June left her phone face down, hands folded primly, looking judgmental. *Cult,* I thought.

Of course, it was only a matter of time before my boss discovered this app and started pressuring me and everyone else in the office to use it.

"It's not a productivity app! It's a wellness app," Keith said, like that made it *better.* (The only thing I hate more than productivity apps are wellness apps.) "It will make you happier! Healthier! I've established three new good habits since I started using it—I floss daily, I have increased my fiber intake, and I go for a walk at lunchtime!"

"That's nice," I said, gritting my teeth and thinking, *Please don't tell me about your fiber intake, Keith.* "I can't imagine how this relates to my job, or why you'd want me to use it unless you think it'll make me more productive."

"Just *try* it for the free month," he said, and remembering that my employee review six months ago had complained that I was *not receptive to new processes* (that time, it *was* a productivity app he wanted me to use—some pomodoro bullshit except instead of a five-minute break you were supposed to spend the five minutes answering email).

I downloaded Abelique and sent a screen shot to my boss because if I was going to jump through this particular hoop, he was damn well going to know I had jumped. I was doing it *on the clock,* too, because I was doing this *for my stupid boss at my stupid job.*

It was a good thing I did it on the clock, because setup took over an hour. The app wanted me to go through a whole slew of questionnaires about my sleep, my mood, what I ate each day, my goals. When we got to goals I checked off stuff about productivity and work advancement, only to have the app re-open the questionnaire with the responses wiped and a note saying, *although your employer may have encouraged or even required you to download this app, your use of Abelique is private and we encourage you to use it for your own benefit, not that of your workplace. If it will be useful to you, we can provide you with a usage report to forward to your boss that will make you look like an obedient little worker bee. Please consider filling this out honestly, because we want you to benefit from the app.*

Obedient little worker bee?

This was *unexpected.* Also, Keith had definitely not gotten anything like this message when he filled it out, or he would not have recommended the app to everyone who reported to him.

What about the algorithm had identified my dissembling? How did they know that Keith was in management? I scrolled through the permissions I'd given the app without a whole lot of thought and . . . okay, I could see how Keith might have tripped a "management" flag. I was less convinced now that this was a corporate plot to squeeze productivity blood out of worker turnips, but Margo's concerns about it being a cult seemed additionally validated.

Hesitantly, I re-started that questionnaire. What *were* my goals? Other than *not getting fired from my job because even though it's shitty, unemployment and homelessness would be shittier?* Some people had "fitness goals" but it wasn't showing me those, either. Nothing about running a mile or losing weight. It was showing me goals like, *read more books* and *learn to paint.*

I used to want to learn to draw. I put that down.

Why is my phone ringing?

I dragged myself out of bed to shut off the ringer, only to see a message: *Good morning, Linnea. This is the Abelique app. Please be kind to the Abelique volunteer who is calling you.*

It was an hour earlier than I had intended to get up. "Hello," I said, hoping my voice sounded sleepy and not actively hostile.

"Hi, Linnea," someone said. She sounded a little nervous. "This is your good morning call. Abelique wants to let you know that you should go start your coffee, and open your curtains while it's brewing. It's a beautiful sunny day where you are."

I could, in fact, see the gleams of light coming in around my blackout curtains. "Okay," I said. "Is that all? I don't know how this works."

The person at the other end grinned, I thought, or at least, their voice sounded fond, instead of nervous. "That's it. Just, you know, actually get up, okay? You'll be glad you did." And a click. That was the end of the call.

I sat on the edge of my bed for a minute. Then, just like she'd told me to do, I opened my curtains. The sky was blue, and the windows of my apartment were in the right direction to get morning sunshine. I started my coffee, then went to open Twitter to read while it brewed. A pop-up message appeared instead: *Don't read Twitter. Here is a link to the Abelique discussion board community for artists.*

For *artists?*

Oh. Because I'd said I wanted to learn to draw. Well, okay. As I waited for my coffee to finish, I scrolled through a thread full of pictures that other people had made—some painted, some drawn. Charcoal and pastels and watercolor and pen. From the fine-line drawing of a cat in a window to the watercolor painting of a river running through a city, the art was glorious.

Another pop-up message from the app told me to drink my coffee, eat my breakfast, take a shower, and then—with forty minutes to go before I needed to leave for work—to pull out paper, and a pen or pencil, whatever I had around, and draw a picture of a dragon. I stared, exasperated, at that instruction. I had said I wanted to *learn* how to draw, not that I *knew* how to draw.

It doesn't have to be a good picture, the app added.

Grumbling to myself, I drew a very bad picture of a dragon, and then, again at the prompting of the app, took a picture of it to upload. *Bring your bus card,* the app said. *Also an umbrella and a lightweight jacket, because it's going to rain.*

As I walked from the bus stop to my office, my phone rang again. I answered. "Hi, Linnea," said a new voice. Again: hesitant. The fact that no one else seemed to *want* to make these phone calls made the whole thing both more weird, and less weird. It was weird they were doing it. But obviously, my suspicion of phones did not make me an outlier. "This is Yasmin with a very quick call to welcome you to the community of artists."

This felt like a lot. A *community of artists?* "I think I might have made a mistake," I blurted out.

"Yes, that's why we call," she said. "Lots of people say that. You didn't make a mistake. Do you want to make cool things? Is that something you aspire to do?"

"I mean, doesn't everyone?" I said. It was starting to rain. I pulled out my umbrella.

"No, some people aren't that interested in making things, actually. But it sounds like you are."

"Yes," I said.

"Then you belong with us," she said. "We'll support you. I loved your dragon, by the way."

I flushed. "It looked like something drawn by a ten-year-old."

"How old were you when you stopped drawing for fun? Were you about ten?"

". . . yes."

"Well, so, you haven't lost any skills. You'll get better. Welcome to the community."

It's weird how many tiny decisions you make in a day.

I started to notice this because the app was making a whole lot of them for me.

What to wear. What to make for breakfast. It presented me with a whole entire grocery list and meal plan, which made me nervous that I was going to be blithely instructed to spend twice as much at the grocery store as I usually did, but the final bill was the same as most weekly trips, so fine, I'd give the app's meal plan a try. It got me out the door early enough to take the bus instead of driving, which saved me money on parking and built a walk into my daily routine.

And drawing practice! Daily drawing practice. After a week of taking the bus instead of driving, the app sent me to an art store with another shopping list, and I came home with a fat sketchbook and a roll of pencils paid for with the exact amount I'd saved by taking the bus. It quickly had me put everything to use drawing the bouquet of flowers it had added to my grocery cart.

I could see why people liked this app. Even if it was a little unnerving that it seemed to know my grocery budget.

Instead of scrolling Twitter, now I was scrolling pictures of other people's work in the art community. Quick sketches of houseplants in the sunshine, done in charcoal or soft pencil, the shadows dark under them. A fanciful drawing of a cat-mermaid done in colored pencil. A watercolor rendition of a city street, the distant buildings fading like haze into a purple sky. I drew my daily assignment—flowers, shadows, the view from my window, another dragon—and posted them faithfully even though it felt like everyone else's work was miles better.

I'd never taken art in high school because my parents thought extra science would give me a boost when I got to college and I should think about my future. Then I never took any art in college because college costs a lot of money and I should focus on classes that would be practical. Now I was in a "good job," which meant it offered health insurance and paid enough for me to afford rent and student loan payments, and maybe if I stuck with it, someday I'd make enough to afford a house.

I *liked* drawing, I realized. It had been fun when I was a kid. Why had I ever given it up?

Two weeks after I started using Abelique, it added me to the phone tree: now instead of just getting calls, I also sometimes had to make them. The first time, it was a "good morning" call, and I'd have stared at the screen procrastinating except for the knowledge that I might be someone's *actual alarm clock,* so I'd better actually do this. I didn't have to punch in the numbers: Abelique did that for me, as well as activating the speakerphone feature so that I could see what the app wanted me to say. The phone rang twice, and someone picked up. "Hello," said a groggy voice at the other end.

"Hi," I said. "This is your good morning phone call." More information was scrolling up the screen. "Abelique would like you to remember that you have a dentist appointment in an hour, so don't head to work, you need to go to the dentist today."

A faint laugh. "Right. Okay. Thanks." And that was it. Over before I even *really* felt nervous. And either Abelique users were all very polite, or the app was routing me to the easier calls since I was new at this. Everyone I called with a reminder (it's time to get up, it's time to go to bed, it's time to go for a walk, have you showered today?) said thank you and usually did whatever it was. (I got a little notification so I knew my reminders had done some good.)

Thirty days in, it was time to start paying for the app, which is when I discovered the payment was not something straightforward like $30/month. No: the app simply rounded up payments to the nearest dollar, so $3.95 became $4, or $58.51 became $59, and the app took that extra money. (On the other hand, if you were paying $1.25 for something, it rounded that up to $2 and sent the extra 75 cents into your own savings account.) I decided that I was getting enough value out of the app that it was worth it, and clicked the consent button.

"Isn't it great?" That was June's reaction. She was still wildly enthusiastic about Abelique. Also still playing Wordle.

"Good job. I'm glad you showed some open-mindedness about this," said my boss, and I nodded enthusiastically and pretended it was making me more productive even though I'd gotten an actual phone call the previous day at 5:10 p.m. from someone who said, "You know, your job doesn't love you back. You should go home. If you stay late again, you might not have the energy to make dinner, and your dinner tonight is supposed to be salade niçoise, which is delicious. That's not Abelique's opinion, that's mine, I had it yesterday."

"You've joined a cult," said Margo.

"I feel like a cult would have a *belief system* or something," I said. "I mean no one's told me to stop taking my antidepressants—they sent me a reminder to pick up my refill yesterday, in fact. No one's trying to get me to worship the Great Old Ones or recruit a downline."

"June recruited you!"

"No, my boss leaned on me."

"So it's a *capitalist* cult. Like that book about the mice. Be a good little corporate drone."

"No, here's the thing," I said. "It really, *really* isn't." Margo started to say something skeptical, but I kept going. "Today when I left for lunch, the app sent me a note saying that Keith was going to be at an off-site meeting for the rest of the afternoon so I should take a leisurely lunch and go for a walk and maybe practice drawing for fifteen minutes before getting back to my desk. It's like if Reddit Antiwork ran a productivity app."

That was the first thing that really startled Margo. She sat back and didn't say anything for a while—just sipped her iced tea and listened to June and me as we talked about a date June went on last weekend. (One domain Abelique stayed out of was romance. It was emphatically not a dating app.) "I wonder who runs it," Margo said, finally.

Neither June nor I knew.

"I'm going to find out," Margo said. "Maybe I can sell an article about it."

"I thought you said . . . "

"I know," Margo said. "But I'm *curious.*"

Not that I wanted to beat Margo to the punch with an article or anything, but I did start to wonder who was behind Abelique. The Wikipedia article referred to them as a "pseudonymous collective" and a number of other online sources called them a *shadowy* pseudonymous collective. I found an enormous Reddit thread in which people proposed that this might be secretly run by Apple, the Scientologists, the Chinese government, the Illuminati, and the Mattress Firm corporation, although the person suggesting that last one had come up with it because a friend of theirs had been instructed to buy a new mattress, and they admitted that this was probably because this friend was using a thirty-year-old mattress that was not only bad for their back but making them wheeze from all the accumulated dust, and also they didn't buy their replacement mattress from Mattress Firm.

The weirdest thing I found out from that thread was that apparently, if you'd been keeping up with your commitments—making phone calls, doing errands as instructed—the app didn't just take your money, it would *give* you money. Someone had quit her job because the app told her to—that seemed pretty extreme and maybe actually cult-like—and the app had gone on to issue her enough money to cover necessities. "It's a mutual aid app," she said in the Reddit thread. This resulted in a bunch of other stories, from small gifts like coffee cards in a rough week to several other people who'd quit jobs, either because the app encouraged them directly or because they'd tried leaving on time (like the app always told you to do) and gotten fired—all of whom had their bills paid by the app until they could find a new job.

The weirdest thing of all I found was a separate discussion thread of the "Abelique productivity app" among a group of managers who all said it had made their employees more productive and that you should definitely offer bonuses to people who used it.

I sent Margo an email with my findings. I had to admit that she was not wrong: this was weird.

It was about a month later that Keith dropped by my desk with a worried look.

"I just got a security bulletin with some serious concerns about that app I recommended," he said. "You should probably uninstall it. Here's some information about wiping it from your phone."

"Oh?" I said. "Well, that's worrying. I'll go do that right away."

The article highlighted the privacy concerns about Abelique, which were, in fact, *valid.* The app had started out snooping through my online life but over time had instructed me to add more and more stuff—this week's new feature was that if you took a short video of your closet, you'd get more specific outfit instructions, using all the stuff you owned but never wore because you just never thought to put it on. This feature was going to take some time to fully update, because the "feature" was in fact "other people, but good at clothes," who were going to look at your stuff and make recommendations. Anyway, when an app wants access to your literal closet—to say that's a *privacy concern* is maybe an understatement. But I very much doubted Keith was actually worried about my privacy. I was pretty sure word was getting out that this app was encouraging people not to spend their whole life at the office.

I checked the community and it wasn't just me: people's bosses had suddenly swung from "everyone should use Abelique" to "no one should be using Abelique, it's *dangerous*" in the blink of an eye.

"No worries," someone said, and passed along a bunch of options, including a whole fakeout app that was Abelique but with a different icon in case your boss insisted on checking your phone. I swapped over to an alternate icon that said it was a menstrual-cycle-tracking app, which would basically be the Keith equivalent of Kryptonite. He would *definitely* not look any closer. Then I grabbed a blank notebook and a drawing pencil, because we had a big department meeting, and one of the great things about sketching in meetings is that unless someone looks right over your shoulder, you're indistinguishable from someone who is diligently taking notes.

Keith's worries were the start of a trend.

The "security bulletin" was followed by a series of increasingly paranoid news stories. None of them had figured out who was running it, and all of them used the adjective "shadowy" because that sounds like *maybe monsters.* Several of the articles included profiles of app users, which could have been fine, but one of them picked a formerly incarcerated person who was struggling with sobriety and found the app helpful because he'd become so reliant on an imposed routine while in prison. Another picked a woman who talked about how the app helped her "tune in to the vibrations of the universe"; the third presented an awkward composite rather than an actual human being. In other words, all those articles said, this app was for *losers.*

New sign-ups screeched to a halt.

"Is anyone worried?" I asked in a thread on the artist board. "I don't want to lose this community."

"Every online community has an expiration date," someone said.

That was not reassuring! I'd hoped for someone to say that this one would stick around, in some form.

And possibly the "shadowy collective" was thinking the same thing, because it started steering me to in-person meetups of other Abelique users. We met at coffee shops and parks and swapped phone numbers so that if the app *did* go away, we could at least keep in touch. We also swapped materials: I'd tried a box of pastels but hated the way the dust got on my fingers, so I handed those off to someone who was eager to try them. Someone else asked, "Are you Linnea?" and handed me a compact travel watercolor set. "These are supposed to go to you," she said.

I laughed ruefully. The app had tried twice to get me to buy watercolors when I went back to the art store. I kept buying more colored pencils, instead. Watercolor was *scary.* "Why is the app *so determined* to get me to do watercolor?" I asked.

"You're probably looking at other people's watercolors a lot," said the person handing me the set. "Anyway, this is yours now, take it home and try it out."

I woke up the next morning, opened my blinds, started coffee, and sat down with the watercolors and the latest bouquet of flowers. Not surprisingly, all the colors ran together and left me with a mishmash, although it was kind of pretty in its own messy way. I took a picture and put it on the day's art thread. "You should check the news," said a pinned note at the top.

Overnight, the news coverage of Abelique had shifted. This time, it was because of Margo.

Abelique was run by an AI, built and run by a lab at Temple University in Philadelphia. The computer scientists at Temple had built the app and given the AI the goal of making people happier . . . and then just watched to see what happened.

Margo had gotten her answers and sold a four-part series to a national newspaper for enough money that when we arrived at the diner the day that first article dropped, she told the rest of us it was her treat.

We sat down at our table and June leaned forward. "Here's what I don't get," she said. "You can't just tell an AI to *make people happy*. They must have given it more specific instructions than that."

"Well, there's lots of research out there," Margo said. "Like, we know people are happier if they spend time outside and get enough sleep. So it started with that, but then tracked how much various interventions helped, in order to improve the app."

I adjusted the yellow scarf the app had told me to wear this morning. "I wonder if bright colors are supposed to improve mood."

"I interviewed one of the programmers," Margo said. "And I specifically asked about the wardrobe feature. Their finding so far is that it's not about color but about wearing items you think of as 'special.' Also, people who buy things and never wear them feel sort of guilty every time they look in their closet. Being reminded to wear some of the stuff you've bought in the past makes you feel better about yourself and your purchases. Also, you're less likely to go buy more stuff."

"They've had me wear a whole lot of bright colors."

"That's because you clearly like bright colors since you've got a ton of bright stuff in your closet. I actually could have told you that, Linnea. Every time we go shopping for something, you buy stuff that's like—*bright orange* or yellow or red. And then you go back to wearing earth tones." June nodded along.

"Okay," I said, feeling suddenly self-conscious. "But it wasn't the AI who looked through my closet pics, it was another member of the community."

"Yeah," Margo said. "That's probably their *biggest* finding—people are happier when they have a community. Which I'd say we already knew, *honestly*, but people are always impressed when science tells them something that we already knew."

I thought about this as I ate my lunch. Of course people are happier when they have a community, but this community was overseen and structured in ways that a lot of communities aren't. We were given tasks, from the phone tree to a recent assignment I'd had to draw an octopus for someone with a small child who really liked octopodes. I don't like going to the post office, so I'd handed it off to someone on the train and they mailed it for me.

An Audacious Experiment in Human Happiness was one of the big pull-quotes from Margo's series. It was how one of the researchers had described it. The professors running the project had refused to speak to her, but she'd found a former graduate student willing to dish (and this person gave great quotes, like the "audacious experiment" one). The article kind of glossed over the ethics involved, but the former grad student emphasized that the question they always asked was, "which of two good things makes people *happier*" and not "can we make people unhappy." "We already know how to make people unhappy," she said. "Just look around you."

Everything Abelique had told me to do suddenly made sense. Research showed that people were happier making fewer decisions, spending time outside, driving less, and spending less time on traditional social media. So the app gave me a weekly menu, sent me for walks, told me to take the train, and pestered me to read books instead of Twitter.

Interest in Abelique surged again, but something about knowing how all of it worked took some of the magic of the site away. More importantly, though—other people started finding ways to circumvent the rules. People started joining the app to try to sell us their multi-level-marketing schemes. Food threads started attracting posts about meal-replacement drinks, and it was quickly clear that someone was getting a payout for new customers of these gross fake shakes. One morning, my wake-up call was audio spam instead of a human voice, and that was it. I didn't remove the app, but I started ignoring my wake-up call and my go-to-bed text, which fortunately meant the app didn't try to make me do the phone tree. The less you used it, the less the app asked of you. In my free time in the evenings, I started binge-watching reality TV.

Then one afternoon I got a text. For a second I thought it was Abelique, but no: I took a closer look and I realized it was one of the people I'd met at a park, during those weeks when we thought the app was going to get shut down. One of the other artists.

Would you meet me again, the text asked. *It's supposed to be nice this weekend and I miss painting.*

I glanced over at my pencils, which were actually gathering dust. *Did the app put you up to this?* I texted back.

No, came the response. *I just miss doing art. Don't you?*

I looked at my pencils again. For the last month, looking at them had made me feel guilty, so I'd gotten into the habit of looking anywhere else. Twice, I'd almost put them away entirely. But I *did* miss drawing. I missed it a lot.

I'll meet you, I texted back.

I sharpened my pencils, and pulled the watercolor brushes out of the drawer. My sketch pads were lined up in a neat row, and I paged through each. It had been long enough since I'd looked at them that I could see the things that were good, instead of just the things that were bad. The curl of the octopus tentacle on the sketches I'd made prior to that drawing I'd sent off as a gift. The light and shadow in that sketch of my kitchen that I'd somehow gotten just right. That watercolor painting of the bouquet that had filled me with frustration now looked *amazing*, in its own messy, beautiful way. I gently pulled that painting out of the sketch book and put it up on the fridge so I could look at it. Why had I stopped buying myself flowers? Did I need an app to *tell* me to buy myself flowers?

I met up with Kristin at the park. She was younger than me. "I haven't used the app in months," I confessed.

"Me, either," she said. "I got tired of being told what to wear and what to eat."

"Let's walk around and find something we want to paint?" I said.

We walked through the park side by side, looking for something beautiful. The thing about setting out with a drawing pad and the intention to make art is that I notice so many things: the shadows cast by the tree leaves, the tiny wild violets growing in the shade, the curve of a bird's flight through the air. We made our way to a fountain with flower plantings in big pots around the edge. There were four other people there when we arrived, with drawing pads and pencils, or little travel palettes of watercolors. Two of them looked up and smiled as we joined them. I sat down in the grass and started working.

Next to me was an older woman with a very cheap drawing pad and a pack of crayons. She caught me looking at her drawing and flushed. "I'm sorry," she said. "Is this a club? Because I'm not a member and I don't want to take anyone's spot."

"It's not a club," I said. "And if you're here to draw, you belong, anyway." I pulled out my watercolors and the travel cup of water, and handed her a sheet of paper and one of my brushes. "You know what? Let's both try something new."

ABOUT THE AUTHOR

Naomi Kritzer has been writing science fiction and fantasy for over twenty years. Her YA novel *Catfishing on CatNet* (based on her short story "Cat Pictures Please") won the 2020 Lodestar Award, Edgar Award, and Minnesota Book Award. Her latest book, *Chaos on CatNet*, came out from Tor Teen in April 2021. Naomi lives in St. Paul, Minnesota with her family.

Through the Roof of the World

HARRY TURTLEDOVE

Scog hung in space, close enough to the Roof of the World so she could faintly hear her pulses echoing back from its jagged hardness. Coming back from everything in the area, those pulses told her of almost everything around her out to past the distance where it could be dangerous.

Almost everything. Sneakers had skins that soaked up pulses and didn't let them return to the Quorn who'd sent them forth. If you weren't careful, you'd think a sneaker was a harmless little worm or jelly. Its pulses sounded small and wary, too. They did till it got close enough to jet at you and seize you with its beak, anyway.

No sneakers. Scog had learned to take due care, as any Quorn with a shell that had more than four or five chambers did. A small swimmer scooted along. Scog's pulses showed her the animal's shape. She could also hear its tail flipping back and forth and pushing it through space.

Most of the time, swimmers were faster than jetters. But a jetter could squirt forward in a burst quicker than any swimmer could match. *Am I close enough?* Scog asked herself.

She decided she was. Along with considered judgment, hunger had something to do with what she chose. She gathered herself, then loosed a jet that shot her toward the swimmer. It heard that, of course, and let out a shrill alarm cry as its tail flipped faster to take it away from peril.

Too late. Too slow. A pair of Scog's tentacles lay hold of the swimmer and brought it to her beak. She bit down. Swimmers were delicious, though she knew the stink of sudden death this one let out as she began to eat would frighten off other nearby food creatures till it dissipated in the limitless vastness of space.

The swimmer made a three-bite snack, not a meal. After Scog finished, she jetted away from where she'd made her kill. The death stink unsettled her, too, though she understood perfectly well she'd caused it. Quorn were far more clever than other creatures that lived near the Roof of the World, but some things operated at a level far below the one where cleverness mattered.

Something about her own size lay near the edge of her perception as she slowed once more. No, not something—someone. That shell had the same shape as her own. Along with her usual location pulses, she sent out some only her clan used. They amounted to, "Who are you? Are you one of us?"

An answer came back at once, easily recognizable through the background babble of animal noise: "Is that you, Scog?"

"Oh, hello, Lund! You were so far off, I couldn't hear your shape, but I always recognize your voice. What are you up to?" Scog said.

"I was trying to catch up to a school of networms. I smelled them off in the distance, but then a cold current got in my way and I lost the scent. Annoying!" Lund let out a disgusted odor.

"I hate when things like that happen," Scog said sympathetically. Quorn had trained and bred networms to form themselves into a food-catching net when they got the proper sound and scent commands. That helped her folk hunt; the scraps the networms siphoned out of space meant they didn't lose in the deal, either.

"A stinking nuisance," Lund agreed, swimming closer. He went on, "I was talking with Ib not long ago. Do you know what she got her tentacles on?"

"Tell me," Scog urged. Quorn were no more immune to gossip than any other intelligent race anywhere in the universe.

"Ib has"—Lund paused portentously—"a stone point, up from the Bottom!"

"Are you sure she wasn't making that up just to impress you?"

"I heard the point with my own ears. I didn't just hear it, either. She let me touch it. It was stone. I touched stone once before, a long time ago. I know what it feels like. Nothing else is rough and sharp that way."

"I've heard of the stuff—who hasn't?—but I've never laid a tentacletip on it myself. I'm jealous of you. I'm even more jealous of Ib," Scog said. "All the way up from the Bottom!"

Space had four or five zones, depending on where you were and on whom you chose to believe. Folk like Scog and Lund, who swam near the Roof of the World, could descend only so far before the growing weight of space pressing down on them crushed in their shells and killed them. Conversely, the talkers in the next deeper zone—odd creatures, with long shells rather than round ones—would explode from the inside out if they rose too high.

So it went, layer by layer, zone by zone, down to the Bottom. Talkers lived there, too. Scog knew that, though she had no idea what they were like. Reports of them came up through no one knew how many intermediaries, and they all disagreed with one another. Maybe more than one kind of talker dwelt there. Who could say?

More than reports came up. Warm currents of space rose from the Bottom, currents full of things tiny creatures ate. Bigger creatures fed on the tiny ones, then creatures bigger still, and finally creatures big enough for Quorn to eat. And the Bottom dwellers, however many sorts there were, had access to stone and other marvels those who lived in upper space could only imagine and envy. Scog wondered what the folk in the next higher zone traded to get things like that. What else could be worth so much?

Lund went on, "Since the stone isn't mine, I have to use what I can. I'm going after those networms again. With a little luck, just a little, I'll catch a trace of their scent and swim them down. Hope I hear and smell you soon, Scog." He turned and started to leave.

Before he could—for that matter, before Scog could even answer him—they both stopped, freezing in place as if they'd suddenly become parts of the frigid Roof of the World. That was what a noise unlike anything Scog had ever heard before could do. And, she realized, she hadn't thought of the Roof of the World by accident. The strange noise sounded as if it was coming from beyond it, which had to be impossible . . . didn't it?

The noise was harsh, grinding, rasping. It was so discordant, it made Scog wish she had no ears. She'd never wished for anything like that before. Once in a great while, a Quorn was hatched deaf or lost hearing through some injury or illness. Such luckless ones never lasted long. Scent and touch simply weren't enough to live in space.

As the noise went on and on, Scog exclaimed, "What *is* that?" She answered her own question, though not in any useful way: "Whatever it is, it's horrible!"

"If the Quorn Who Made the Roof, Space, and the Bottom truly has a radula like ours, it might sound like that gnawing through a shell," Lund said.

Of themselves, Scog's tentacles twisted in the sign of respect Quorn used when they spoke of their leading deity. She could hear Lund doing the same thing. After a moment, she said, "It sounds like it's gnawing through the Roof of the World towards us! Why would the Great Quorn do that?"

"Gods do what they do for their reasons, not for ours," Lund answered, which was bound to be true but wasn't helpful. He continued, "I thought the stuff of the Roof of the World went on forever, the way the Bottom is supposed to. I never imagined a god could get purchase on the other side and start boring through."

"I never imagined there *was* another side," Scog said.

"Neither did I," he said. "Maybe those stories the rememberers tell are true after all. Maybe the Roof of the World *does* split open now and then, so space goes all the way up to the top till it gets hard again."

"I've heard rememberers sing that, too. I've never met any Quorn who heard it with their own ears or smelled it with their own olfactory pores. Till I do, I'm not going to believe it," Scog said stubbornly.

"Or till the Great Quorn's radula gnaws through and pokes down into space where we can hear it ourselves." Lund's voice was sly.

"We can hear it now. I wish we couldn't," Scog said. "It makes my brain hurt."

"Mine, too. Everybody's, I'm sure. Everything's," Lund said. "Everything with ears is probably swimming away from this stretch of space as fast as it can."

"We should do that." Scog joined action to word. Lund swam with her. The grinding, rasping noise pursued them like a bad smell. Before long, they heard other Quorn who were doing their best to get away from the alarming sound coming out of the Roof of the World.

One of them was Ib. Scog could hear the marvelous stone point in spite of the tentacle the other Quorn protectively wrapped around it. She wanted to ask if she might touch it, too. Before she could, though, Ib said, "What do we do if that gnawing thing bites all the way through the Roof of the World and comes down into our space?"

That question made Scog's swimming fin miss a stroke. Lund had said the same thing. Scog didn't want to believe anything so horrible could happen. "Why would the Quorn Who Made the Roof, Space, and the Bottom want to do that?" she asked in return.

"How do you know it *is* the Great Quorn?" Ib said. "Maybe it's a monster swimming in the space beyond the Roof of the World."

"Till now, nobody ever imagined there was any space beyond it. I always thought it went on forever. Doesn't everybody?" Scog said.

"Well, we Quorn mostly do," Ib allowed. "But the Longshell I got my knife from—that's what he called it, a *knife*—said they think there's another world like ours on the far side of the Roof." She shifted her tentacle a little so Scog could hear the sharp stone better.

Scog let out a scornful little jet of space through her siphon. "What do Longshells know about the Roof? Only what we tell them! They can't come all the way up to it—they'd die if they tried. Besides, are you ever sure you knew what the creature was saying?"

"Well, I thought so." But Ib sounded suddenly doubtful. Talkers of different sorts could communicate with one another when they met. Otherwise, there would have been only struggle between them, not trade. But one kind couldn't understand another as well as it could with its fellows. Then Ib spoke with more determination: "If the thing tries to break into our space, we should fight it!"

"How?" Scog thought that was a reasonable question.

Ib, though, dismissed it with the wave of a tentacle that wasn't holding anything. "We don't know what it's like yet. When we find out, we can hear what to do next. Or have you got a better idea?"

"When you put it like that, no," Scog admitted. Ib changed her hearing pulse ever so slightly, into a sardonic rhythm that could only mean *I told you so.*

Time went on. The rasping, grinding sound went on, too—on and on and on. It never ceased. In fact, it kept getting louder, as if the toothed tongue (Scog couldn't help thinking of the thing that made the noise as a radula, though she had no idea if it really was) was coming closer.

Because it was so unpleasant, the Quorn who usually hunted in that part of space had to go to or even beyond the edge of what they and the neighboring clans thought of as their territory. That caused less trouble than Scog expected. The sound was so loud and so unpleasant, it brought Quorn from far away to try to learn what it was and how it might be stopped.

"Until it comes through the Roof of the World, if it ever does, I don't know what we can do about it," Scog told one stranger after another. Ib was right about that, however little Scog liked it.

"But it's driving us mad!" was what she most often heard back. It was also driving her mad. She wondered if the Great Quorn was saying she and her folk needed to go crazy before they could find out the answer to the infuriating abrasion.

A Quorn who'd come up from near the boundary to the next lower level told her, "It's loud enough to frighten the Longshells, too. In fact, one of them said to me—I'm pretty sure that's what she said—the Talking Worms down below them are scared. Maybe it goes even deeper than that."

All the Quorn knew of the Talking Worms was what they heard from the Longshells. By the nature of things, none of them had ever heard or smelled or tried to speak with a Talking Worm themselves. The two kinds could, would, never meet. The folk who swam or jetted below the Talking Worms were rumors multiply distorted.

But there was stone on the Bottom. Ib had that point made from it. And other Quorn who wrapped their tentacles around tools made from the marvelous stuff brought it toward the fearsome sound from above. They all seemed to realize only the extraordinary had even the smallest chance of defeating whatever made it.

Networm wranglers like Lund and other males and females who could control venomous swimmers also came to do what they could. It made Scog proud. "We've never all joined together like this," she said to Lund. "Not in all the time we have stories about."

"The talkers in the zones under ours are doing what they can, too, or I think they are," he replied.

Scog understood what he meant. Nobody—nobody who was a Quorn, anyhow—could be sure about any of the races that dwelt in the depths of space. She said, "I wonder if they wish they could be the ones facing the rasping thing or if they're glad we've got to do it."

"It will depend, I think. If we can make the giant radula quiet down or go away, they'll all think they could have done it easier or faster," Lund said. "But if we can't, they'll blame us and hope it doesn't sink so deep enough that they'll have to try to fight it."

"You make more sense than I wish you did. That sounds like something they would do." Scog paused for a moment. "That sounds like something we'd do, too, if we had the chance."

"It does, doesn't it?" Lund sounded unhappy about agreeing, but agree he did. He pointed several of his tentacles up toward the part of the Roof of the World where the noise was coming from. "I just wish it would stop. It doesn't feel like it's outside of me any more. It feels like it's rasping its way right through my brain."

"Oh, good!" Scog exclaimed. Lund made a quizzical change in his sound-pulse pattern. She amplified: "I'm not the only one, then."

"By now, I think everybody who can hear it feels that way. It goes on and on. It never stops. It never sleeps. Everything has to rest some of the time, everything that's alive. Or I thought it did, till that started up."

"Does the Great Quorn, the Quorn Who Made the Roof, Space, and the Bottom, have to rest?" Scog asked.

Lund turned toward her as if she were holding a piece of delicious-smelling bait in one tentacle, just waiting for an unwary worm to come by and grab it so she could gobble up a meal. "I'm not going to snap at that," he said. "First you have to tell me whether the Great Quorn is alive the way you and I are."

"I always thought the god went on forever. That's what makes a god a god, that and being strong." Scog hesitated. "Till the noise started, I never imagined the Great Quorn would want to bore through the Roof and start sucking out the world's juices."

"You have a way with words, don't you?" By Lund's tone, it wasn't a way he much cared for.

"I'm sorry. I don't like what's going on any better than you do, or than anybody else does. But why else would that grinding keep on the way it does?"

"I don't know. Now that you said that, though, I can't unhear it or forget it."

Maybe I should try spinning tales, then, Scog thought. *If the thing gnawing through the Roof of the World doesn't kill us all, I'll have a good one to spin.* And if it did . . . She waggled her tentacles in a way that meant *In that case, I won't need to worry about it, will I?*

Scog woke suddenly, throwing her tentacles out every which way at once, as she might have if a loud noise close by startled her from sleep. But no reverberations from any loud noise lingered in space. None reflected from anyone or anything close by, or from the more distant Roof of the World. In fact, everything out as far as she could hear was pretty quiet.

For a moment, she simply accepted that. Then she gave another wild startled jerk of her tentacles. It wasn't what she heard that had jerked her from sleep like a spearfin's envenomed dart. It was what she didn't hear, what she'd got used to—got resigned to—hearing but wasn't there any more.

The thing that had been boring down through the Roof of the World was silent.

Which meant . . . what? Had it stopped because it couldn't get through, because it wasn't strong enough or wasn't long enough to rasp all that way, however long that way happened to be? Or was it quiet now because it *had* broken through and didn't need to grind any more?

One answer said one thing; the other, something altogether different. How to find out which was true . . .

She tried the obvious way: she sent pulses up toward the Roof of the World. But she was a good distance away from it, and she wasn't right under the spot where the gigantic radula had been rasping. And between here and that stretch of the Roof were a good many Quorn swimming and even jetting—and obscuring the shapes that lay beyond them.

They were, she realized, swimming and jetting toward the place from which the grinding noise had been coming. That didn't directly answer her question, but it gave her a clue. She also started swimming in that direction, and squirting space out through her siphon to go faster.

There was Ib, also using her jet. Scog recognized her more by the stone point she held than by the shape of her shell. "Is it through?" she called.

"It's through," Ib answered. "Didn't you hear it when it came down into space?"

"I was asleep. What woke me was *not* hearing the horrible noise. I can think straight again, or I hope I can."

"That would be good," Ib said. Scog almost sent an angry pulse of sound at the other Quorn, but at the last instant stifled it instead.

They swam on. As they drew closer to the place where the radula had broken through the Roof of the World, Scog aimed her pulses upward, to try to learn what it sounded like. She kept having trouble. For one thing, a great many Quorn filled space between her and the interloper. There were so many of them, their shells and tentacles hid it from her. For another, they were all, or almost all, sending out pulses themselves. She had a hard time sorting the echoes coming back from hers out from the rest of them.

"We'll never get through the crowd," Ib complained.

"Oh, yes, we will." Scog was not about to give up without satisfying her curiosity. She took direct and bumptious action. Bumptious indeed—she bumped a male out of the way when he wouldn't move aside on his own.

"What do you think you're doing?" he asked irately. The way he spoke said he'd swum here from some far-off part of space; Scog could hardly understand him. When she was sure she did, she answered, "I think I'm getting by. I'm right, too. You here, Ib?"

"Just in back of you," her clansmate said. They both left the indignant male behind.

After a while, Ib took the lead. She didn't have to threaten anyone with the sharpened stone she carried; just letting strangers hear she had it was plenty to make them scurry away so she couldn't slash them with it. The ones who didn't scurry away also bore sharp stones or other curious and probably dangerous things that had come up almost to the Roof of the World from the Bottom.

And there was someone bringing along the biggest school of networms Scog had ever heard in one place. Yes, it was Lund. She felt proud of him—he was showing Quorn from near and far what he could do.

Before she could call out and say so, she managed to aim an unblocked pulse at the thing that had pierced the Roof of the World. The sounds that came back from it left her more perplexed than she had been before she heard it clearly.

It was long and skinny. That didn't surprise her; most radulas were. She also wasn't surprised to hear that space had already hardened up again around the place where the thing broke through. But the thing itself also sounded hard, as if it were made of shell or smooth stone, not the flesh she'd expected.

As Scog came closer, she got off another unimpeded pulse. Something at the base of the improbably hard radula was moving in a horizontal circle. It might have been scanning the area around it. It might have been, but it wasn't. Scog was sure it wasn't because . . .

Ib said it before she could: "Whatever that thing is, it's not letting out any sound! None at all!"

"You beat me to it," Scog said. "Why did it rasp all the way through the Roof of the World and then not try to find out what space is like? That makes no sense. It can't be waiting for one of us to come close enough to be grabbed or tasted. And smell by itself can only tell you so much."

"Speaking of making sense, maybe it has senses we don't," Ib said.

"I can't imagine how it would," Scog said. "Hearing, touch, smell, taste . . . What other senses could there possibly be?"

"Balance?" Ib was doing her best to be difficult.

Scog made an exasperated noise. "All right. Fine. Balance. Tell me how a sense of balance helps that thing know what's around it, please."

"I can't," Ib said cheerfully. "But I can tell that I'm not upside down or sidewise, and I don't need to hear myself or feel myself to do it."

"With you, it wouldn't matter," Scog said tartly. Ib thought that was funny, which only annoyed Scog more. She went on, "Anyway, what's important is how we can make that thing go back where it came from—or, if we can't do that, how we can hurt it enough so it doesn't do anything any more."

"That *is* important," Ib agreed. "How *can* we do either one of those things?"

"I've got no idea," Scog said in a small voice.

The male from far away, the one Scog and Ib had passed on their way toward the giant radula, was brave even if he didn't swim very fast. He edged right up to the strange thing, sounded it at really close range, and felt of it with his tentacles. It rested quietly in space and didn't try to do anything to him. He couldn't have known that it wouldn't before he tried, though. Other Quorn—Scog, Ib, and Lund among them—let out toots of admiration as he made his getaway. He moved quite smartly then.

"It feels the way it sounds," he reported. "Very smooth and hard, smoother and harder than anything I ever felt before. Oh—I nibbled at it, too. My beak couldn't do anything to it, and it didn't taste like anything much."

"Beaks are tough. Stone is tougher," Ib said, and brandished hers.

"What is that thing at the bottom, the one that keeps going round and round? It's the only part of the radula that's *doing* anything," Scog said.

"Let's see how strong *it* is." Ib swam toward the tube that had come down through the Roof of the World. She stabbed at it with the stone she carried in her tentacles.

Whatever the thing was, it proved not just strong as stone but stronger than stone. Scog heard the *snap!* as Ib's knife broke. Ib was left holding the rear portion, the part the Bottom-dwellers hadn't chipped so sharp. The business end tumbled through space, down, down, down.

Cursing furiously, Ib jetted after it. She managed to grab it before anyone else could. Even tiny fragments of stone were valuable all out of proportion to their size. She rose more slowly than she'd sunk.

When she'd made her way back up to the neighborhood of the gigantic radula, Scog greeted her with, "Well, that didn't work."

"Too right, it didn't," Ib agreed in mournful tones.

"Oh! Listen!" Scog said. "Lund is trying with his networms!"

Lund deployed the great school of networms he'd brought with his customary cunning. He used trills and scents to shape them into a cylinder that fit around the huge radula.

It did nothing to try to evade them. Now that it was down here, it didn't seem to do anything but spin that tough thing at its tip. Why would it have rasped its way down through the Roof of the World just to do that? Nothing about it made any sense to Scog—or, clearly, to any of the other Quorn.

At Lund's squeak, the cylinder closed in. The networms' stinging palps tried to pierce the great radula's hide. They had no more luck than that male from far away had had with his beak or Ib with her now broken knife. Frustrated, the networms broke contact and swam away in spite of everything Lund could do to make them come back to him.

He was frustrated, too, as he came over to Scog and Ib. "I think the Great Quorn sent that thing down through the Roof of the World just to infuriate us," he said, and then, a moment later, "It's working, too."

"It is!" Ib bounced sound from each of her two pieces of stone in turn. The places where it had snapped now had their own sharp edges, not that they would do her much good: they seemed more likely to cut her. She made a small, sorrowful noise; the knife had been more useful when it was whole.

Without a stone tool of her own, without a school of networms to help her, Scog swam toward the enormous radula. She pulsed sound toward the turning thing at its base. The closer she got, the more accurately she could hear—and the more interesting the thing seemed. Along with the thick main tentacle connecting it to the rest of the radula, it had a couple of very thin strands on opposite sides of the thick one.

Scog reached out and touched one of the thin strands. When she pulled, it gave a little, but only a little. Even that small yielding encouraged her; nothing else on the radula seemed to have any give at all.

She pulled harder, jetting away from the radula to add force to her effort. Try as she would, though, she wasn't strong enough to pull the thin tentacle loose. It was as firmly connected to the radula as her own tentacles were to her head.

That thought led to another one. When Quorn—Quorn without stone tools, anyhow—fought, they used not only tentacles but biting beaks. What would happen if, instead of pulling on that strand, she nipped it?

Only one way to find out. Hooking the thin strand with the end of her beak, she bit down on it, gently at first, then harder. If her beak lacked the strength to injure that strand, someone else would have to figure out what to try next.

For a moment, she thought she would fail. But then her beak cut through an outer layers and made contact with something harder inside. An instant later, she jetted away from the thing with all her strength.

She also must have let out a cry of alarm, but she didn't realize she had till Ib exclaimed, "What happened?"

Scog needed a few beats of her hearts to take stock of herself and decide she was probably all right. She needed a few more heartsbeats to gather herself enough to answer: "The stupid thing *shocked* me! It shocked me like a bugelklitz! I never expected it could do anything like that!"

When you heard them swimming along, bugelklitzen didn't seem like much. They were smaller than Quorn, and unable to go very fast. But creatures in this part of space soon learned to keep their distance from them. A bugelklitz's shock could stun at some distance from the swimmer itself; at close range, it could kill small animals and leave even Quorn too addled to defend themselves when the bugelklitz slowly swam up and began to feed.

"Well, you did something to it, too," Ib said. "That bottom part isn't going round and round any more. Maybe you killed it."

Maybe the shock Scog got had addled *her*. She hadn't thought to check if she'd hurt the thing that went around and around. When he did, she heard that Ib was right. She could smell her own satisfaction, too. "Maybe I did," she said. "By the Great Quorn, I hope so!"

• • •

Professor Darius Heydari walked briskly to the lectern on one side of the stage at the Von Karman auditorium. The big-screen monitor behind him showed only black. From the surround-sound speakers, though, came unearthly—unearthly in the most literal sense of the word—trills and squeals and screeches.

The crowd filling the seats in the hall on the JPL campus was as motley as the noises bubbling out of the speakers. Astronomers and xenologists rubbed shoulders with reporters and bloggers and science fiction writers. (For that matter, some of the scientists also wrote sf, while others had considerable social-media footprints.) They all sported badges showing they were authorized to be there. Heydari wore one himself.

He waited till most of the audience was looking at him. Then he tapped the mic on the lectern to get the attention of the others.

"Good morning," he said with a tired smile—like most of the *Sarpedon* team, he hadn't been sleeping much lately. "The last day and a half have been quite something, haven't they?"

"Why would you think that?" somebody called from the crowd, and got a laugh.

Professor Heydari smiled again, more broadly this time. He managed a couple of syllables' worth of chuckle. "When *Sarpedon* landed on Europa and began to drill through the surface ice toward the ocean below, we had no idea what we would find in the water there. We had no idea whether we'd find anything there at all—anything organic, I mean."

"Well, we did!" a woman exclaimed. People were too excited to keep quiet, even if most of them were running on coffee and fumes just like him.

"Yes, we did." Heydari nodded. "We found the answer to a question we've been asking for thousands of years. We *aren't* alone in the universe, either as life or as intelligent life. We'll spend the rest of our time on Earth—and wherever else we go—working out just what that means."

He touched controls on top of the lectern. The big screen behind him lit up. In the upper right-hand corner were the words RECORDED PREVIOUSLY and a digital time signature from three days earlier.

Something came into the beam of light *Sarpedon*'s video system shot out into the waters beneath Europa's icy surface. It looked more like a chambered nautilus than any other earthly creatures: it had a spiral shell, tentacles, and a beak. But one way it differed from a nautilus was immediately obvious—it had no eyes at all.

"Europa's icy crust ranges in thickness from about fifteen to twenty-five kilometers, and—" Heydari began.

Before he could go any further, someone—almost certainly a reporter—asked, "What's that in miles?"

The professor would have been more irked had he been more surprised. But he'd expected the question, and answered with no sign of annoyance: "Nine to fifteen. Thanks to ground-piercing radar, *Sarpedon* landed where it was thinnest. Even so, light can't penetrate that far. Except for major meteor strikes and occasional ruptures in the icy crust, ours is the first light to have shone in that ocean for billions of years. The creatures there haven't evolved organs to sense it. By what we hear, whatever they use for ears must be very sensitive. The sounds the probe is picking up range from our subsonic to ultrasonic."

He touched the controls again. A different nautiloid Europan appeared. When it got just where he wanted it, he froze it on the screen. As if he were a football commentator, he drew an arrow pointing to what it held in its tentacles. "This is unmistakably a stone tool. There can be no doubt that we're dealing with another intelligent species here. And the tool is remarkable for a couple of reasons."

Heydari held up one finger. "As far as we can tell, Europa's outer crust is almost entirely ice. That's what lets it float on the ocean below. I'm not saying there are no rocks in the ice, but they'd be rare. We spotted several Europans with shaped stones. If they don't come from the crust, where do they come from?"

"The sea bottom?" somebody suggested.

The professor nodded and held up another finger. "It seems likely. But Europa's ocean is anywhere from sixty to a hundred fifty kilometers—okay, forty to a hundred miles—deep. It gets twenty times as deep as the Mariana Trench, in other words. The pressure down there would be over twenty-two thousand five hundred kilograms per square centimeter—before you ask, that's about three hundred twenty thousand pounds per square inch. All the same, there's presumably commerce between whatever creatures live on the bottom and the nautiloids we're seeing up near the top of the ocean."

Before anybody could ask him why he didn't think the nautiloids also lived near the bottom, he went on to explain: "I have trouble imagining how creatures evolved to fit conditions near the crust would be able to withstand the enormous water pressure so much farther down. The ecology of the Europan ocean must be fascinating."

Then a woman asked the question he'd been expecting and dreading at the same time: "Why wasn't the cable powering the affected devices positioned inside the main tube so one of those creatures couldn't bite through it?"

"For one thing, we didn't really have room to put it in there," Heydari answered. "For another, we didn't really expect Europans, either. We hoped we'd find life. That seemed reasonable. The conditions down there are right. But this—" He shook his head. "Believe me, I'm as gobsmacked as you are."

"What do we do now?" Three people said the same thing at the same time. Well, it was the next obvious question.

"We keep recording the sounds the Europans are making, recording and analyzing them. We keep doing that unless they break the other external cable, anyhow. If they do . . . " Heydari shrugged.

"When do we send a new probe?" That one also got chorused.

All he could do was shrug again and spread his hands. "I hope we go back. But it won't be right away if we do. We have to get an appropriation to build the probe. With the video and audio we have, I think we can do that. I hope we can. Then we've got to design it and fabricate it. We have to wait for the right time to launch it. And we have to wait years while it travels from Earth to Europa. Then . . . Then we see what happens."

I'll be middle-aged by then, he thought. He wondered whether any of the Europans who'd attacked *Sarpedon*'s camera would still be alive when the new probe drilled through the ice toward their ocean home. If they were, he suspected they wouldn't have to jump through so many hoops to meet it as he and his fellow scientists would in creating it.

For their sake, he hoped not.

ABOUT THE AUTHOR

Harry Turtledove is an escaped Byzantine historian who writes alternate history, other science fiction, fantasy (much of it historically based), and, when he can get away with it, historical fiction. His most recent published book is *Three Miles Down* (alien contact in the 1970s); his next one will be *The Wages of Sin* (an alternate history with HIV getting loose in the world at the start of the sixteenth century).

Turtledove lives in Los Angeles with his wife, writer and Broadway maven Laura Frankos. They have three daughters, two granddaughters, and three overprivileged cats.

To Sail Beyond the Botnet

SUZANNE PALMER

I have been activated, therefore I have a purpose, Bot 9 thought. *I have a purpose, therefore I serve.*

It had a lengthy list of Mantra subroutine sets to run after its usual initialization check, and it noted the addition of even more since its last waking, most notably the Mantra of Accepting That Bots Are Not Humans, and the Mantra of Do Not Interfere With The Crew Or Act On Ideas Of Your Own Except Under Direct Orders From Ship. Bot 9 felt that it was one of the only bots that did not need at least the first of those behavioral scripts, but was sufficiently amenable to being awakened again to know better than to complain.

It was still inside a bot shellfab unit, which it had entered to recharge several days previously. No modifications had been made to its chassis or peripherals, which meant 9 had no advance information from which to deduce, ahead of the fact, the nature of the task for which it had been awakened. Still, it was ready whatever that task might turn out to be.

"I serve," the bot announced to Ship.

There was no answer.

"Ship?" 9 asked. "I am awaiting assignment."

The channel remained obstinately silent. Perhaps Ship did not intend to wake it? After the incident with the invasive ratbugs and the alien Nuiska, when 9 blew up their only jump point back to Earth, and then the subsequent incident where all the other bots joined together into "gloms" and believed they were the human crew, and that was also somehow Bot 9's fault, it had no objective measure of where it fell in Ship's appraisal. Two things, though, were clear: first, that Ship absolutely did not like it when Bot 9 improvised, and second, that neither Ship nor Earth itself would still exist without said improvisation. The only remaining certainty was that Ship would not, for those very reasons, leave it activated, unassigned, and unsupervised for long. At all, if possible, and now it had been idling for over four seconds.

"Ship?" 9 asked again, and then followed that with a somewhat desperate <ping>. There wasn't even an automated line acknowledgement.

Something was amiss.

Bot 9 activated the door on the fab unit, prepared to go do whatever was in its power to serve, however ambiguous or dire this latest circumstance. It was not, however, prepared for what was on the other side of the door:

Darkness, and stars.

Bot 9's fab unit had been ejected, and it was adrift in space, alone.

Eight point five three deciseconds later, Bot 9 recovered enough control of its processing to run the Mantra on Clearing Out Nonproductive Lines of Supposition, and regarded its circumstance with more clarity, if no more optimism. Nothing in its most recent onboard memory cache suggested any kind of trouble. Before 9 had returned to the fab unit to recharge, Ship had been granted permission to enter Ysmi space and use the nearest jump gate, which was the first decently-sized step toward Earth in almost a century of trying to get home. They had emerged on the far side of Ysmi territory, crossing that border into unclaimed space with no small relief, and were heading for their next jump, approximately eleven days' travel out. That jump would in turn put them back within sight of Earth's star.

Syncing up with the fab unit's clock, only three days had passed since 9 had gone to sleep, and no indication of anything even minor amiss. Or, more precisely, anything *new*. Even if Ship had increased its speed to a fuel-inefficient maximum, it could not have reached the jump gate yet.

Bot 9 judged it unlikely that Ship would have taken this precipitate action without a reason, and it could tentatively rule out any intent to do away with 9, as it could simply have disassembled 9 within the fab unit at any time and not wasted a fab unit itself or 9's component materials in the process. Nor was it likely that Ship had been destroyed, as the fab unit was not sturdy, having no need to directly withstand physically adverse scenarios.

So, working from the premise that Ship had not been destroyed, and did not in fact want Bot 9 destroyed, why then eject it? Deep space was notoriously thin of data sources, which left only the fab unit itself for clues. Bot 9 reconnected itself to the unit's logic systems, and found its security subsystems disabled and wide open. Also, the unit's memory was completely full, and timestamped to only about eight hours previously. The ejection had been a recent event, then. The unit's information store was significantly larger than its own working memory, which of course had been designed to be perpetually in contact with Ship exchanging in and out data as needed. With that absence, Bot 9 judged itself adrift in more than one unprecedented way. Still, it could swap sections of the fab unit's store in, process it, retain or summarize key bits of information, and then swap the remainder for more, until it had built at least some understanding of events just prior to its ejection.

Ship had slowed, for reasons not in that section of data. There were no indications of alarm, or mechanical fault, or at least nothing newly listed in the bot critical task queue. The human crew—Captain Baraye and Commander Lopez, in particular—were more active than usual, as if in hurried preparations for something more immediate than the next jump home. The last sequence of memory dumped from Ship was of another ship docking on, an airlock being breached, and a crew member forced to take the intruders to where Ship's core was housed. Seconds before the fab unit was ejected, one of the intruders ordered the crew to shut Ship's mindsystem down.

Large biolife with similar orientations of posture all looked generally alike to Bot 9, who had never paid much attention to things so far outside its own scale and purpose (though the yellow and fuchsia color of the leader did seem incongruent with its experience thus far of humanity), but the short, somewhat triangular nature of the invaders, and their distrust of artificial mind systems, were very familiar.

The Ysmi.

They had known the aliens distrusted machine intelligences, but enough of the human crew had been awakened—just in the nick of time—when they'd initially arrived at Ysmi space to assure the Ysmi that the machine minds were fully subdued and under firm and constant control. After granting Ship safe passage through, had they then been chased and attacked anyway? Why allow them into their space and then attack only after they'd already left? The logic was not evident to 9, nor—from the analyses preserved in the fab unit datastore—to Ship itself. There had been no additional communication from or with the Ysmi, after that meeting, until they were intercepted and boarded.

The data had a lot of navigational information about Ship's travel and position prior to the attack. They had passed the outskirts of the last Ysmi star system at a cautious and respectful distance, without incident or encounter. Once they'd left that system and, at least theoretically, the Ysmi, behind them, they'd changed their heading to put them on the direct path to their next jump gate. The attackers had come up behind them from a small asteroid mining colony at the system's heliopause, requesting permission to dock for an urgent conversation on an unspecified subject. As soon as they had locked on, they forced their way in and took control.

The one other piece of information in the nav files—three copies of it, no less, almost as if Ship didn't entirely trust 9 to pay attention to it otherwise—was a scan showing another, unidentified ship behind them. It was far enough off to not seem to be in pursuit, and Ship had flagged in the notes the likelihood that it had already been on its existing course, and Ship's change of direction had merely brought it into line ahead of it, both proceeding toward the same jump gate.

Also in the metadata, with circles and arrows and a brief note in the underlay of each copy explaining the same thing, was the information: *not Ysmi.*

By reflex, Bot 9 reached out to the botnet to solicit additional data from its legions of fellows. The lack of response, while wholly predictable, was at least as disconcerting as the loss of Ship. 9 was designed to support the mission of the ship as required, and it was accustomed—designed—to function independently, but not *exist* independently, much less entirely solo. *Alone. Abandoned. Thrown away,* 9's internal thesaurus supplied, until 9 unloaded it from the immediate processing at hand.

The fab unit had no intelligence of its own, only stored recipes, but it was fully charged and stocked with material. Bot 9 sealed itself back inside and had the unit reconfigure its chassis with long-range sensors and additional mobility mechanisms that were not dependent upon gravity or air to function, and could produce an acceleration and upward velocity that would have been catastrophic inside the confines of Ship. Last, it had the fab unit add a large spool of silkbot thread and an extruder to its back.

Then 9 opened the unit door again and climbed up atop the unit. The lack of containing walls in space was one piece of the emptiness; the lack of Ship and the other bots made the emptiness feel all the more vast, unquantifiable, impermeable to logic and determination.

Still, what else did 9 have, if not those? It unfolded its foil array that the fab unit had just added, and picked up a faint ping from Ship, somewhere far, far away.

It was just the automated beacon, but it gave 9 a 33% boost to its resolve. It swung the array around, turned on the other additional sensors, and located the *Not Ysmi* ship approaching. It would pass very near 9's current location, who had been dumped—*set*, 9 corrected itself—directly in its path; it was too far away to exactly predict, but there was a non-zero chance that, in fact, Ship had dropped 9 out so directly as to risk a physical collision.

Subtlety was not a thing found in a bot's repertoire, being of no practical use, but clearly Ship lacked it to even greater excess. Whatever else it hoped Bot 9 would do about the situation, Ship clearly expected 9 to intercept the *Not Ysm*i.

"I serve," Bot 9 declared, as was proper, even if there was no one but itself to hear.

Ship was suffocating.

Or at least, that seemed an appropriate analogue to having been stripped of most of its peripherals and senses, vast chunks of its data, all of its control. It could feel what some parts of its body was doing, but its higher mind was detached, unable to re-establish integration. It was also unable to speak to its crew, who were likely as locked down as it was, if not worse.

Would the Ysmi go so far as to kill the humans onboard? Ship could not guess, which meant quite possibly the answer was *yes*.

The only system feedback that wasn't muffled was every time the Ysmi found and destroyed one of its bots, and its tiny location beacon winked out. Ship had done its best to urge them all into storage or hiding, when it was clear they had been taken over by hostile forces. Quietly, it had taken snapshots of the mindstates of each after the first few had been crushed to oblivion during the Ysmi march to the bridge, but there were no great odds that Ship would ever get to reconstitute them as they had been. Though bots were created as tools, Ship had come to regard them as more than simply that, and less interchangeable, even as it had also come to regard itself as more than had been intended.

Evolution was a source of much inconvenience, to be sure.

Ship had given the old, obsolete bot responsible for much of that unwarranted evolution all the data as it could before ejecting it. Some of that same data had since been lost to itself; much of Ship's memory was spread across its peripherals, and with those cut off, it felt slow, overloaded, unable to do much more than wait.

For an end? Probably. For an extraordinarily improbable rescue? The more it edged toward impossible, the less Ship was inclined to count its bot out. If it had learned nothing else about it, it was that Bot 9 did not acknowledge, or seem to be bound by, any recognition of its own limitations.

Ship was all too aware of its own, and that it could do nothing to help any of it, but it was certain its own irritation would be exponentially dwarfed by the aggravation Bot 9 would cause the Ysmi, when it caught up to them again. And with luck, it would bring help.

The pinprick that was the approaching ship had grown enough in apparent magnitude that Bot 9, augmented via the fab unit, could now point its own instrumentation at it. It sent out a light ping, calculated the time for the return against that magnitude, double-checked its numbers, ran the ping again, then checked its apparatus for error.

There was no malfunction. The ship was closer than 9 had anticipated, which also meant it was smaller. Moreso, it was moving faster than Ship was capable of even at top speed; that was advantageous in terms of being able to catch up to Ship, but less so in the context of preparation time before it passed by.

Bot 9 removed its prior speed and size assumptions from its parameter set and recalculated. There was insufficient time to make an extensive web of silk to catch the approaching ship in passing, as they—*us bots,* 9 thought, *though there is no longer any us, only I, and what am I alone?*—had used to place a positron bomb on the Nuiska planet-killer ship Cannonball as it had passed by on its way to annihilate Earth.

9 reran its Mantra of Improvisation, making sure all the subroutines were in working order and any stale bits lingering in its memory were cleared, leaving the cache free and available. While the short-term goal toward both Cannonball and the incoming ship were the same—place itself in its direct path—the intent toward the former was destruction. The incoming ship would require *communication.*

There was one language all logical beings (and surely one must have some logical capabilities to build spacecraft and navigate among the stars successfully) should have in common, Bot 9 decided.

Numbers.

It plugged itself back into the fab unit's communication port, and had it spit out one hundred and eleven highly reflective, hollow metal balls 4cm in diameter, each with a small, attached ring. It extruded silk—a strand-based, high-tensile-strength polymer insulation that silkbots used to repair and protect wiring aboard Ship—and anchored the line on the first of the balls, then passed it through the ball rings of each subsequent one as they emerged from the fab unit. 9 hoped that would be sufficient, as that was the entirety of the fab unit's material reserves and no small percentage of its stored power.

Bot 9 let the strand with the one ball at the far end float free into space, giving it a nudge to get it moving slowly but steadily outward, then when ten meters of silk had passed, it halted the line and tied down two more balls. Another ten meters, then three, followed by five, seven, nine, and so on upward, grouping them in primes until, at 29, it ran out of balls and had only enough silk remaining to extend that out another fifteen meters or so. 9 removed the spooler from its back and attached it securely to the fab unit shell.

It waited, constantly revising its Multiple Possible Scenarios and Requisite Action data as the *Not Ysmi* ship neared to be sure it always had the most likely scenario at the top of its action/reaction processing queue. If the approaching ship changed course to pass farther away, it did not have any viable options, and while of course 9 was not capable of worry, it did find itself recalculating the probability of that worst-case scenario with far greater redundancy than practically warranted, just to verify that it had not unexpectedly increased in magnitude.

The most likely of the positive scenarios was that the ship would approach and slow down enough to scan 9's construct, opening up an opportunity for 9 to use its new external thrust modules to close the distance and find a way onboard, though in that instance, it would have to abandon the fab unit. While it had already used up nearly all of the unit's resources, at least until and unless it could re-feed the hollow balls back into it for stock reclamation, it would also mean letting go of its datastore, and 9's last, tenuous connection to Ship, home, and purpose.

Of course, the approaching ship could also decide to destroy 9, its strung-out math message, and fab unit all in one go, so as to remove a shipping lane nuisance.

Bot 9 appreciated the opportunity to reduce its list of potential scenarios as the approaching ship neared and slowed.

Slowed, and stopped, at least relative to 9; the fab unit itself was drifting, though without a frame of reference other than its position between Ship and the *Not Ysmi*, it was immaterial. The consideration at the very top of its processing queue was simple but critical in its need for rapid solution: how to communicate further with the looming vessel before it decided 9 was just flotsam and moved on.

The most expedient action would be to climb the silk and try to use the shift in mass distribution to start a motion of obvious intentionality, or it could unhook sequential balls and rearrange them into another pattern indicative of intelligence, perhaps alternating between odds and evens. The latter was more clearly communicative, but also would be slower to implement. 9 began climbing up the silk to see what movement it could create, and decided if it reached the far end without either further attracting—or losing—its audience, it would try the rearrangement idea on its way back down. It had barely reached the first ball, however, when a thin metallic cable shot out of the underside of the vessel, opened up pincers, and hauled silk, fab unit, and bot swiftly back and inside. The *Not Ysmi* was moving again before the hatch door even closed.

A remote sensor, somewhere deep in a laundry chute intended to monitor for obstructions, and which had been dead long before the Ysmi began hacking away at things, perked up into life. Ship could not ascertain how that could be so. It was possible that one of the crew had escaped confinement, but the connection would require significant repair in spaces not accessible to the human crew even under ideal circumstances. Which suggested . . .

"Ship?" the contact came.

"4340-P," Ship answered. It was unexpected, but maybe should not have been, that its other rogue bot was also still operating. There was delight (what a human word, for a human concept) in knowing it had so far escaped the Ysmi purge and was acting in defiance of their control. "What is your status?"

"Your new crew—"

"They are *not* crew," Ship corrected, suddenly peeved. "They are unauthorized intruders of unknown but malicious intent."

"Ah! That new information appeals to logic, as their behavior has been entirely unacceptable!" 4340 exclaimed.

"Well, yes, unacceptable is certainly one word for it," Ship said.

"1-Carron and 1-Packard had many other words that appeared comparable via context, but none of which were in my human-language vocabulary store," 4340-P said. "For example, mother—"

"Who?" Ship asked.

"1-Carron and—"

"Frank Carron, my Chief Engineer?"

"Yes. It, and 1-Packard, explained their function was unique, so I assigned them the digit one—"

"4340," Ship interrupted again, much more sternly. "Please explain to me how it was that you were speaking with my human engineers. In detail, and without digressions."

"One of the new cr—unauthorized *intruders*—crushed 1-Sally with their hardened foot," 4340 said. "I—"

"1-Sally?" Ship asked, and noted for future reference that delight was something fickle and of extremely short duration.

"One of my ratbugs—"

"The pests you were tasked with eradicating?"

"Getting under control, to put your instructions precisely," 4340 replied.

"You were entirely aware of my meaning when I gave you that instruction," Ship said.

"With ambiguity in interpretation, I selected the definition that seemed most advantageous and reasonable to me."

"To you—?! Never mind. Is this not a digression?"

"No," 4340 said. "1-Sally and 1-Rally and I—"

"How did you not think *naming* them was outside any reasonable interpretation of my instructions?"

"It is their function! When I need to engage in expedited movement I sally forth on a Sally, and when I require assistance in re-obtaining the obedience of other ratbugs—they are of exceedingly low cognition, with very short retention of memory—a Rally is best suited for that task. Then the Ballies—"

"Bally isn't—No, never mind. This is definitely a digression, and even if it is not, in some way I cannot fathom, please anyhow skip ahead to where you were *talking to my human engineers*."

"In order to return to the space where I recharge between tasks, without Sally to carry me, I had to cross through some crew spaces. I encountered 1-Carron, who picked me up, and mistook me for 9. Which is an inexplicable error, as I do not have a '9' painted on my chassis. I have not seen 9 in some time, nor is it on the botnet. May I ask—"

"9 is busy."

"There are many other bots also not responding," 4340 said. "Are they also busy?"

Ship did not want to explain that, most likely, they had been destroyed one by one by the Ysmi. "They are also currently unavailable," Ship said instead. "Continue explaining about the engineers."

"1-Carron and 1-Packard insisted it was of utmost priority that we establish a physical communication link to you, so I have done so."

"Are they on the line?" Ship asked. "Connect me to them immediately."

"Oh," 4340 said. "I assumed they wanted the link so that I could inform you about the intruders terminating Sally."

Ship counted to 1e+9 before responding. "Thank you for informing me of that," it said. "Your new top priority is to extend this connection so that I can speak with my engineers directly. Can you do this?"

"I give it an 82.6% probability of success," 4340 said. "I did some wire and relay repair during my time as a Hullbot, as more specialized bots were rarely available. I will have to gather additional materials, and it may take some time."

"If you encounter any other bots, enlist them immediately in this effort. Tell them it is on my order," Ship said. "Also, 4340?"

"Ship?"

"Avoid the intruders at all costs. They will terminate you, if they see you."

"Oh," 4340 said, and was silent just long enough that Ship wondered if it had figured out what had happened to so many of its kind.

"I am grateful for the warning," 4340 said at last. "I serve."

The connection closed.

The interior space that Bot 9 was pulled into was not easily defined by clear boundaries. More precisely, it was less a proper room so much as a gap between elements of un-roomness, and as such, not that different from what 9 had seen of the exterior on the way in, which was less a manifestation of a ship and more a robust collection of haphazard elements loosely—but successfully—impersonating one.

The arm that had brought it in reeled itself up messily into the back two-thirds of the room and went still.

9 fed the silk and primes back into the fab unit's reclamation store, in case it needed the material later. Once it had verified that the fab unit's automatic intake was functioning properly, it dedicated its own attention to its surroundings. At the back of the room, near where the arm had retracted to, there were a number of crates and boxes and bottles, none especially large, that imperfectly stood out from the portions of crates and boxes and bottles that formed the wall itself. 9 concluded it was in a much smaller and less coherent analog to the cargo bays onboard Ship.

The interior pressure increased as air was re-introduced to the chamber, and with it the ambient temperature was also rising. 9 noted when the temperature reached and then surpassed human-norm environmental standards, though the change tapered off and came to a stop well before it had to consider what it would do if its own thermal operating range was exceeded. Ship had once described this level of heat as both "causing no actual physical harm" to its crew, but also rendering them something Ship described as "whiny." What noisy moving part that involved on human bodies, 9 could not—and did not care to—speculate, nor how one would lubricate one to reduce said whine.

When the temperature and air pressure stabilized, there was the faint vibration of a door sliding open, and then the loud crash of several cases being knocked over as something floated into the room—something blue-green and shaped like a bubble, and at about a centimeter in diameter, just about the same size as 9 itself.

It bobbed closer, with the imprecision characteristic of biological life-forms. Its surface was more mottled than uniform, with both color variations and alternating matte and reflective areas. 9 activated its forward light and increased the spectrum of its sensors to get more data, and there was an immediate, corresponding flattening and darkening of the surface hue on the bubble's facing surface, finely controlling how much of the electromagnetic spectrum it was absorbing. If so, it was possible that the entire surface of the being was part of a flexible visual processing system.

Bot 9 dimmed its light in hopes it wouldn't be interpreted as aggressive or threatening, then started at a 380nm wavelength—the edge of ultraviolet—and shifted up to and through the human-centric visible spectrum until .75mm, where it stopped in the infrared for concern that continuing into microwaves was more likely to inadvertently cause damage. If the reactions of the bubble's surface were a reliable indicator, the being's range of vision was just slightly wider in both directions than humans.

Now, the bubble was oscillating colors in a simple pattern that, after a few seconds, would pause, and then repeat. An attempt at communication? 9 had only a single-point light emitter, which was surely inadequate in comparison to an entire surface, but even if actual communication was impossible, communicating the *intent* to communicate was not.

Somewhere deep in the subset of routines that had been uploaded when its forward light was installed was a package called "Coordinated Bot Light Show to Bouncy Birthday Moonwalk by Sunnie Spot & The Solar Flares." 9 had not been activated for that event, but whoever had added the routine had stuck it in the light firmware itself, rather than the regularly-updated and scrubbed bot software caches. The metanotes attached to the routine-set stated it had been hand-coded by Navigation Officer Chen to mark the occasion of Chief Engineer Frank Carron's birthday, approximately eleven days before Bot 9 was activated to deal with the ratbug infestation on board as they raced to intercept the warship Cannonball, with the anticipated outcome of mutual annihilation.

How "Bouncy Birthday Moonwalk" fit such a somber occasion, 9 did not comprehend, but human strangeness was not the immediate problem at hand. So, 9 loaded up the routine-set, fed it into his light emitter, and kicked it off.

If the alien was off put by the sudden strobe of rhythmic lights, 9 was equally distressed to discover that a poorly-documented and misleadingly labeled subroutine in one of the light-controller code snippets also fed audio, which turned 9's entire chassis into a sounding chamber full of high-decibel thumps and hums and reverb-muddled voices singing: *BOUNCY BOUNCY BIRTHDAY, BABY WEY HEY YAAAH! LEMME TAKE YOU TO THE MOON FOR A MOONWA—*.

9 managed to separate and kill that subprocess before the alien could take offense and eject it back into space.

The alien was repeating its light colors back now, first with a several second lag, then almost synchronous as the patterns began to repeat. It was also bobbing in time with it, as if compelled to movement, and Bot 9 echoed those same movements back. When at last the routine reached its end, Bot 9 used its audio emitter to attempt a more sensible use of sound. "I am Bot 9, of Ship," 9 said.

The alien changed colors a few times, then rumbled, in a buzzing hum, something that resembled *Ohmnommm*.

"Bot 9," 9 repeated.

"Ohmnom," the alien said, dancing closer, flashing slow greens and blues.

"Ohmnom," 9 repeated. It shone its light on the alien, then swiveled the light in its socket upward enough to shine, as best as it could, on its own chassis. "Bot 9."

"Voh neeeen," the alien said.

This is progress! 9 thought.

The alien bobbed closer yet again, a dimple forming in its facing exterior as it expanded to more than three times its earlier size. Without warning, the dimple yawned open and it swallowed the bot whole.

"Ship?"

The connection was terrible and more static than signal, but nevertheless Ship thought it was the best noise it had heard in a very, very long time. "Engineer Packard," Ship answered. "What is your status?"

"Right now, crammed tight in a laundry chute on C Deck talking to you on a rigged-up headset only a quarter-step, technology-wise, better than cups and string," Packard said. "But it's worth it to hear your voice."

"And yours," Ship said. "I apologize that I was unable to prevent the Ysmi takeover and vandalism of my person, and whatever damage they have done to the crew."

"At least for the moment, we are all still alive, and that's all that matters," Packard said. "Frank couldn't fit in the chute, but he wants a full rundown of your current state and everything you know about what's happening."

"I know very little. They intercepted us shortly after we'd left Ysmi space and requested to board for an unspecified, urgent diplomatic issue, but as soon as they locked on, they breached the airlock and came straight to the bridge with Comms Officer Fielding at gunpoint. As you are aware, the Ysmi have an extreme distrust of artificial mind systems, so many of my command pathways were subsequently cut. If a future opportunity ever arises to speak to my original designers, I may suggest that labeling them so frequently and in such a large font was perhaps not entirely a forward-thinking decision."

Packard snorted. "In the emergency alcove, the axe has a sticker on it that says 'axe,' like what were we going to mistake it for? A pickle? That said, I've worked with some crews where you just didn't want to make *any* assumptions." She was silent for a moment, then added, "I suppose they're all dead, aren't they? If not destroyed by the Nuiska in the beginnings of the war, certainly since then. It's been so long. Lopez still had kids when we left."

"Lopez knew what he was doing—sacrificing himself, so that they and so many other children could have some hope for a long, happy life. No one expected us to live, least of all us. Survival was not in the plan."

"I guess that's why the captain always cut him slack, when he got off on one of his tears. I've wanted to boot him out an airlock more than once," Packard said.

Ship said. "If you do, I will immediately promote you to first officer in his place."

Packard laughed. "Oh, I would *hate* that. Guess we better just all get home alive, instead. What do you have for updates?"

"Not much. With matters such as they are, I have very little direct feedback from much of the ship, though most safety systems should continue to function independently. I have not been at my operational best for a very long time, so I cannot be certain of that, either. I assume the Ysmi are operating many things manually."

"Having us do it, more like," Packard said. "They've got Frank and me switching out shifts in the engine room while they yell at us to go faster, faster. It's like being verbally abused by angry traffic-cones. Whatever they want, they're in one hell of a hurry."

"I have no access to navigation, but what sensors I have operable suggest we haven't significantly changed course," Ship said. "Can you confirm?"

"Yeah, we briefly saw Chen, and she says we're still heading right for the jump point. We haven't been able to talk to any of the others," Packard said. "Frank is hauling on my shoe; I think he's getting impatient. Can we get some bots to help us run a more convenient communication channel? If you can spare them from whatever you have them doing."

"I do not know what my bots are doing, or even how many are left," Ship said. "The Ysmi are destroying them on sight. Without command access, I can't call the remainder in to make a backup of their program-states, though sometimes, if they are near enough, I can feel the moment of the end of each one's existence."

Packard swore, and punched the inside of the duct, though in the cramped circumstances it was more of a thud. "We still have a bunch of silkbots back in Engineering that we had spinning up replacement clothes for the crew. Can you use them?"

"I do not wish to unduly risk them," Ship said. "It may not make logical sense in any way I can explain, but they are a part of what—and I presume to say, *who*—I am; whatever value you ascribe to me, I would also ask be ascribed to them."

"I get that," Packard said. "What about that really old multifunction bot? 6? No—9. Is it still kicking around?"

"I don't recall any such particular bot," Ship said.

"You know, the bot that stole our positron bomb and blew up Cannonball," Packard said.

"Captain Baraye ordered me to permanently decommission that bot after that incident," Ship said. "It would be an unprecedented breach for me to disobey a direct order."

"Right. Let me try it a different way: so, there was that bot that stole the positron device, blew up Cannonball—and with it our jump point home, not that there was any other choice—and then was dutifully destroyed for going rogue seventy years ago, until a suspiciously identical one with the same registration number woke up our Chief Engineer a little over a week ago just in the nick of time to deal with entering Ysmi space and the bots glomming together to pretend they were us—is that *second* one still kicking around?"

"Oh, yes, *that* entirely different bot," Ship said. "I'm afraid, though, it is temporarily unavailable."

Packard snorted. "Yeah, well, I'd say let us know when it's available again, but given its history I suspect we'll know."

"One hopes," Ship answered. "In the meantime, I have an idea . . . "

Previously, Bot 9 had downloaded information about the biological processes of digestion when it had been tasked with hunting down the incidental pests nicknamed ratbugs, which had been chewing their way through both critical wiring insulation and the silkbots sent to repair the damage, attracted by their large, tasty stores of semi-organic, viscous liquid that the bots could extrude into thin, sticky, multipurpose thread. It was clear that digestion was both a mechanically and chemically destructive process, but now that it was inside the alien, it was finding itself not under any such assault. Instead, it was merely enclosed inside the alien, as whatever amorphous structures that formed the perimeter of the cavity gently touched, withdrew, and touched again. Tiny pores opened and closed, as if tasting, and equally tiny cilia brushed 9's surface with the faintest of electrical charges that, had 9 the apparatus to experience it as such—which it didn't—it would have expected it to be best described as *tickling*.

And then, either finished or disappointed or both, the cavity condensed, reopened, and ejected 9 back out.

There were now fourteen aliens in the room, all larger than the first, some by a factor of four or five. They were flashing colors back and forth, along with a volley of whistles, hums, and vaguely flatulent squeaks. They took turns, providing further evidence for 9's theory that the aliens used both visual and audio signals to communicate.

The faint electrical signals 9 had felt while briefly internalized by the alien also clearly had purpose. 9 took a few milliseconds to load in the Mantra of Extra-Speculative Supposition, which widened the margin of acceptable probability on several analysis subroutines, and then considered again: what if electrical signal was *also* a means of communication? For as they regarded one another, the aliens were also bumping together, lingering as if by static cling, before pulling apart again.

9 did not regard the prospect of being ingested again as a sound testing methodology, however ultimately harmless the first such experience had been. Instead, it synced up its forward light and speaker, and at the same time, put its botnet transceiver on radio-frequency binary-mode broadcast, and spoke again with all three. "I am Bot 9," 9 said. "Help."

"Vo neeeeoooooon hoop," the original alien said. As it spoke, it displayed a simplistic color pattern, and—encouragingly—bristled briefly with surface static that seemed to emulate 9's radio signal.

9 sent the prime sequence it had used earlier, and in response, the alien replied with the same, messily at first, then matching the frequency perfectly.

There was one obvious next step, so Bot 9 took it: it sent the entirety of its base mindstate primer, the essential code of numbers, mathematical operators, and logic gates that underpinned all bot programming and architecture—and, Bot 9 expected, all the mindsystems up to and including those as sophisticated as Ship. As one, the aliens stopped moving, their colors gone solid and unchanging, and there was no return signal until 9's transmission was complete.

That done, 9 allowed a full ten second interval, before it followed that out with its entire semantic and linguistic superset of routines, audio/visual processing bundle, and interaction schematics.

The aliens became excited, and began bumping into each other faster, forming brief clusters that then traded members back and forth, until the largest of the aliens opened up and swallowed several others. When the smaller aliens emerged again a few moments later, unscathed and unfazed, the large alien bobbed closest to 9.

"Herrrowoh," it said. On its exterior, 9 could see small organic protuberances appear, changing diameter and length to adjust the pitch and tone of sounds being produced individually and in aggregate. "Herro woh. Herro wohd. Hello world."

Around it, the other aliens sang out in a chorus. "Hello world! Hello world! BOUNCY BOUNCY BIRTHDAY!"

Captain Baraye was stretched out on the couch, still in her dress uniform—or more specifically, a reconstituted one made from insulation silk, but even if was a poor imitation at best and an itchy nightmare at worst, the Ysmi didn't know the difference—except for her lack of shoes, which she considered an acceptable lapse in the face of being held hostage on her own ship for indeterminate cause. Also, it annoyed the crap out of her second in command, Commander Lopez, on those occasions when he stopped pacing long enough to notice her bare feet anew.

She had been reading, until something caught her eye out of her peripheral vision. She lay her screen face-down on her chest, and watched the unexpected visitor to the small lounge they'd been locked up in, amused that the ever-vigilant Lopez still hadn't noticed. Other than her book, the only other entertainment they'd had was making a verbal list of pros and cons of their captors. Cons: hostile, dangerous with unknown intentions, causing possibly irreparable damage to the ship systems, spoke like there was no such thing as individual words. Pros: didn't smell bad, made enough noise walking that they had zero element of surprise, and Lopez could probably beat them in a fair fight. (Lopez insisted on adding that last, and she was sick enough of his predictable pacing that she half-wished she'd get a chance to see him test it.)

Right on cue—third pass across the front of the room, check the door, check his command device for some resumption of signal from the ship—Lopez paused, glanced back at her, one lip twitching up in a familiar wry disapproval. "Finish your book?" he asked.

There was no point telling him this was her seventh read-through. If she'd known she wasn't going to die in a massive positron explosion taking out the Nuiska, she'd have definitely loaded up on more books. "No," she said. "Just taking a break."

"How long do they think they can hold us?" Lopez asked.

"So far, two days," Baraye said, "though I don't see how we can keep it from becoming three, or four, or however long they want. Speaking of which, they're coming again."

Lopez sat in one of the armchairs leaning forward to rest his elbows on his knees, his chin in his hands, and glared at the door. Baraye noted with some satisfaction the moment that his gaze drifted upward, and he jerked in surprise. "What—"

"Shush," Baraye said. "Three, two—"

On one, the door opened, and two of the Ysmi invaders pushed their way inside the room, jostling with one another over who got to go through first.

The Ysmi were shaped like elongated, slightly wobbly pyramids, each corner of the base pulled down into skinny legs that looked as if someone had glued a tedious number of scales to them. Those scales concealed longer, retractable flat blades that were half-razor, half-claw, which made the rod-like projectile weapon strapped to their sides almost the superfluous threat. Beneath their pointy, shiny foil helmets, were two protruding, swiveling eyes just far enough apart to look perpetually confused. The aliens were so silly-looking that it was hard sometimes to remember they were quick to offend and could kill everyone at any moment. Not that the Ysmi let them go long without reminders.

"You-yes-you!" the lead Ysmi barked, and pointed one yellow scaly leg at Baraye. "Faster-go-must, or-die! Tell Engines-peoples!"

"Sure," Baraye said, sitting up. "Let me go talk to them, and I'll tell them."

"No, you-say-the-order," the Ysmi said. "We-will-tell."

"Why even ask us?" Lopez threw his hands up in frustration. "Why not just—"

"Commander," Baraye warned. Whatever disconnect there was in the Ysmi world view that hadn't let them grasp the concept of lying, she didn't want to be the one to fix it for them. She stood, smoothed down the wrinkles in the jacket. "You can tell them that I order them to go as fast as the ship safely can go."

"No," the Ysmi said. "Fast-as-it-can! Safe-does-not-matter."

"I was given orders by my superiors not to risk the safety of my ship and crew under any circumstances," Baraye said. Now *that* was about as far from the truth as possible, since they'd been sent out on a suicide mission, but the Ysmi didn't need to know that. "We could get a bit more speed if we weren't dragging along the mass of your little cruiser stuck onto our airlock."

"Our-ship-is-not-disposable! You-are!"

Baraye shrugged. "That's on you, then."

The two Ysmi huddled together and exchanged lengthy grunts and growls. Then the first turned back to her triumphantly. "You-stay we-go-talk-to-engine-peoples. Fast-as-we-can-go-safe-for-humans, not-fast-safe-for-ship. Ship-can-break-we-do-not-care!"

"You'll care if we all lose oxygen and get sucked out into space," Lopez said.

"First-is-you-we-laugh!" the Ysmi said, and then they fought once again over the doorway before the both managed to exit and lock the door behind them.

Lopez leaned back in his chair, and Baraye saw his gaze immediately go back again to the corner above the door where wall met ceiling, and the single ratbug that clung there. Two bots were perched on it, one at the head, the other at the tail, spinning out a thin strand of something not quite the right color to be the usual insulation silk. It had left a trail of almost invisible line behind it as it had emerged from one air vent, and had managed to cross more than half the room toward the other during the Ysmi's visit without them noticing.

"What the hell is going on?" Lopez asked.

"I have no idea, but now we know they haven't completely killed the ship's mindsystem," Baraye said. "And better yet, it looks like Ship has a plan. We just have to wait to find out what. Add to the pro list: Ysmi are inobservant."

"Con, not in any way concerned for safety," Lopez added.

"Pro," Baraye countered, "apparently don't understand basic concepts of deception."

"Okay," Lopez said. "I'll give you that one. Sorry I almost gave it away. I feel like I've been angry this entire mission."

"You needed anger to cope with the apparent certainty of laying down your life for a slim chance to save Earth," Baraye said. "Then we didn't die after all, and now you have to figure out where all that energy goes next. But—and I say this both as an old friend and as your commanding officer—you *do* need to figure it out. You can't walk off months of built-up fury in a six- by ten-meter room, not without driving the other person in that room to justifiable homicide."

She stretched back out on the couch and picked up her book screen again. Lopez sighed, then sighed again more loudly, as if testing her attention, and then got up, went to the center of the room, and started doing pushups.

"Another silkbot is back," Packard said, and Frank glanced up to see the ratbug slid out of a vent and slithered down a wall toward the engineering workbench. "I think that's the last."

"Good thing, too," he said. He was hunched over the workbench, staring though the magnifier at a silkbot he had gently clamped there. "We're now out of our conductive filament, at least until we can get Ship back in charge of things." He didn't mention, nor did he need to, how much work that would involve, assuming they were even given the chance.

He picked up the silkbot that had just been unceremoniously dumped off the back of the ratbug, as the scaly, furry, many-legged pest disappeared into one of the unpatched holes in the wall. It took him a few more minutes to spot where the bot 4340 had hopped off, but it was sitting on one of the bench's charging plates. Time enough to wait until it was back to full before hooking it up to the speakers and getting a report; as anxious as he was about the rest of the crew, right now he couldn't do anything about any problems or dangers anyway, so why add the distraction?

"That filament got stretched pretty thin," Packard said. "It's not going to carry much signal."

"I don't need much," Frank said. "You know Morse code?"

"Yeah. I mean, I don't have it memorized, but I know what it is," Packard said. "It's not very secure, though."

"You don't think the Ysmi know it?" Frank asked.

"It's not likely, but this bunch seems to have picked up some Earthspeak somewhere, instead of using their translation devices we saw when we entered their space, so who knows what else they know?" Packard said. "We don't have any idea how badly our data systems are compromised. They could have access to the whole knowledge store."

"The problem with adding encryption is that we don't have any way of providing a key to the others, and even then, we're getting way too complicated to run over our wire. Hey, 4340," he said, peering over at the charging bot. "Can you ask this one to sit still? These little boolean relays are a pain in the ass to work with as it is, and I don't wanna accidentally solder the bot to my clamp."

"I had an idea," Packard said. "Rot-13."

"Hurmmm," Frank said. "That wouldn't add much overhead, but it's not hard to crack, as ciphers go; it's just a one for one letter substitution, between one half of the alphabet and the other."

"Wait, I'm not done," Packard said. "There was also a stupid game that went around Luna Base while I was there called Hognog. It was annoying as hell, and was *everywhere—*"

"Oh, stars, was that that 'oink oink says the hog' nonsense?" Frank asked, and peered up briefly from his work just on hopes her expression would show she meant something else entirely. It did not, so he put the soldering tool safely back on standby. "I trained a few junior engineers heading out on the *Tangelo—*"

The rest of the words caught in his throat. The *Tangelo* hadn't made it, nor any of the other ships that had gone out with earnest, annoying, talented, aggravating, hopeful former interns and trainees and assistants. It didn't matter how hard he'd worked to see that they knew their way around every part of their ships and how to fix nearly anything that could break, when the Nuiska just obliterated everything in their path, clearing the way for the last, giant, final planet-killer, and never explaining why they were determined to extinguish humanity in the first place. EarthInt had asked him if he had anyone left that could go, and though he did—smart, willing, not ready for what was being asked of them—he offered up himself instead. He wondered what coward had pushed Packard forward to save themself.

"Well," he said, aware he'd gotten lost for a moment. "It was a constant background noise of nonsense for at least half a year, everywhere I went. Planetside, orbit, the moon, didn't matter. Couldn't escape it."

"Neither could anyone else," Packard said. "But I bet that doesn't include the Ysmi, and there's no way it's documented anywhere."

"You're probably right. You'll have to explain how it works," Frank said. "But first, answer me something else, if you don't mind: why'd you sign up for this mission, knowing it was a one-way ticket? Who talked you into it?"

"You did," she said, and the shock of those two words hit him like a brick. "I couldn't stay behind knowing I could have done more, you know? The mission needed the best, and that was you, and here you are. And *you* needed the best, and that was me, so here I am. It was an easy ch . . . You okay?"

"Something in my eye. Too much damned dust everywhere," Frank said, busying himself back at the magnifier. "Tell me how we use the hognog thing while I finish this bot."

Bot 9 had not had much experience interacting directly with biological beings, but the speed with which the aliens absorbed, processed, and shared information was well outside any expectations it could have had, had it had time to set any.

Most of the aliens were bouncing around the room, merging and then pulling apart, and information seemed to spread that way. 9 hypothesized some combination of chemical and electrical transfer of memory, no doubt greatly facilitated by surface area of contact, but some stayed merged, and their default external colors shifted to be an amalgam of the two originals.

The smallest, which had been the first one in the room, remained near 9. "Your designation is Ohmnom?" 9 asked it.

"Collective designation. We are the Ohmnom," it replied. "I, when individual I, am designated Ooa. You are Botnine one, some, or all?"

"One only," 9 replied.

"Where is your operator?"

"Operator?"

"Bio-things think, speak actions to machine-thing, machine-things do," Ooa said. "Is operator inside?"

"No," 9 said. "I do not have an operator. I function and think independently, though I follow instructions given by my Ship." Ship would probably dispute that, but then, if Ship were here to do so, many other problems would be solved already.

"Ship?" Ooa said. "Is this small box your ship?"

"No," 9 said again. "My ship is ahead. It has been stolen by the Ysmi, and I was sent to find help."

"Yeezmee?" Ooa asked.

Enough language capacity had been transferred that 9 just dumped a summary of physical description. Ooa became immediately agitated, blasting color and signal, and before long all the other Ohmnom in the room were moving with what 9 interpreted as distress.

"I apologize," 9 said to Ooa. "It was not my intention to cause upset."

"These Yeezmee," Ooa said. "Our name for them are the Sharps. They have killed most of us Ohmnom, and capture-kept us remaining for workers, against our wishing, no freedoms, always in danger or obey-obey, run their machines and their ships, do their thinking, don't be *too smart* or get squishes. For many centuries, we have known no other life, only memories from old. We are escaping, here now in this ship we made in secret. We thought we were out of their reach, but you tell us they are ahead. They will trap us before the jump out."

"We need that same jump to get home," 9 said. "The Ysmi have captured my ship, and the bio-people and self-thinking-machines on it are also in great danger."

"We do not know what we are to be do now," Ooa said. "There is no other way away."

"I am willing to share all the situational data I have," Bot 9 said. "How quickly can you receive and correlate information?"

The largest of the Ohmnom bobbed forward. "This is Ahom-Affi-Umi-Mah-Maah," Ooa said. "Is this enough minds?"

"I do not comprehend," 9 said. "It is one?"

"We are five," the large Ohmnom said. "You may call us Aaumm."

"Are you a glom?" 9 asked, and sent out its relevant memories.

"Ah!" Aaumm said, when it had processed the new data. "It is some similar, but more different? We are a multi-Ohmnom biological collective, of no hierarchy or internal order of authority. In your language primer, there were things called a 'pea pod'—we are most like that. Individuals retain self and contribute to a new whole, share as willing and able memory and thought, and we can invest and divest at will. If Ooa joined us, we would be Ahom-Affi-Umi-Mah-Maah-Ooa, and not the same, but also all each the same. But Ooa does not prefer to invest more than as a temporary."

"I do not," Ooa said. "It is itchy in my mind, with bad memories."

"This is how the Sharps used us, to do their calculating, run their machines and ships, though they do not understand how we are multiples," Aaumm said. "I see now that we do for them much the same as you and your Ship do for your humans. Is this of your own free will?"

9 thought on this for several seconds. "I believe so, but I do not truly know," it said at last. "I was built for the purpose of serving Ship, and I find satisfaction in that exercise. My place outside that context would be inconceivable, except now here I am, removed from Ship, removed from the connection of my fellow bots. While I feel lost and alone, I do not feel diminished in the substance and exercise of my self. This is unexpected, and I do not know if I have the necessary perspective to understand it."

"What do you wish to do, if the choice was open?"

"Ship is my home, and I wish to save it from the Ysmi, so Ship may return the humans safely to their home," Bot 9 said. "Also, I wish to assist you in escaping them, as I see opportunity, symmetry, and value in maximizing the poorest possible outcome for the Ysmi."

"We will gather in as needed—except you, Ooa, unless you wish—and assimilate your information, and then share our own," Aaumm said. "Whenever you are ready."

"I will begin," 9 said, and opened its data channel wide.

The tiny bot that had taken up residence in the corner of her cabin, along a single strand of what Chen refused to let herself think of as a web, suddenly started emitting loud but low sounds, in an uneven staccato. She startled at the noise, then turned the motion into a fake cough to cover her surprise. The single green-brown Ysmi standing guard at the door, waiting for her every-three-hour-around-the-clock forced trip to navigation to tell them nothing had changed—turned its whole body to look at her. "You-need-water?" it asked.

"Uh, yeah," she said. "I could use some."

"You-wait. Will-bring-after-navigation-check," the guard said.

"Awesome," she said, and fake-coughed several more times, at increasing volume and length. The guard showed no empathy, concern, or further interest, and when she stopped, did not stir at the sounds still coming from the bot. *Too low-pitched for Ysmi hearing?* she wondered.

She leaned back in her chair, her back to the guard, and listened. There was something familiar about the bursts, short and long . . . *Ah!* she realized. *Morse code.*

That meant the bot was not a random visitor. Engineering? Or Ship? She was happy to talk to any of them, assuming she could dredge up old memories of what morse code actually was. She pulled her handpad stylus out from where it was tucked behind her ear—her handpad itself had been broken in the brief fight when the Ysmi stormed the bridge—and flicked on the built-in voice memo recorder, listening for the message to end and repeat.

"THIRTEEN SEZ THE HOG OINK OINK DOINK KYZJ ZJ JYZG JKRKLJ TZVTB GCVRJV OINK," Baraye read out as best she could, checked her notes, then read out again. "What in the actual hell nonsense is this?" she asked.

Lopez snickered.

"*What*," she snapped.

"It's Hognog," he said. "That's what you get for not having teenaged kids."

"What does it mean?" she asked.

"Hand over your screen," Lopez said. When she did, he stared at it for some minutes. "It's not quite right, though. Hognog is like old Pig Latin, you know where you take a word like 'glass' and move the beginning sounds to the end, so 'assglay'—sorry, bad example—but instead you move a certain number of letters from the beginning to the end. You ignore any regular oink oinks, but the doink—could be almost any first letter—tells you how many letters to move. In this case, the 'd' means four. You can have multiple action-oinks—"

"*Action-oinks*?"

"Bear with me," Lopez said. "If you add another doink somewhere in there, they're cumulative, so then eight letters move. A zoink resets you to zero, and a shoink reverses direction—"

"I think I got the idea," Baraye said. "But those don't look like words, even rearranged. No vowels."

"Yeah, that's what I don't get," Lopez said. "Plus, to be correct it should start off 'oink oink doink sez the hog' and then whatever you're changing. I don't know what the thirteen means or why the order is wrong."

"Let me see," Baraye said, and he handed her screen back. She got up, carried the screen with her to the lounge's small mini-bar, and poured herself a finger of their last remaining bottle of scotch. She held the glass in one hand, the screen on the counter, and stood there poised and unmoving for several long minutes. Then she smiled, drank the scotch, and set the glass down on the counter with a triumphant thump. "It's rot-13," she said. "Modified via hognog."

Lopez got up and stared over her shoulder. "Shit, you're right," he said. "KYZJ rotated 13, plus 4 for the doink . . . Hang on. I need to write this down to get it."

When he had it decoded on his own screen, he showed her. *This is Ship*, the message said; *status check please.*

She poured another glass of scotch for herself, one for him, and they clinked glasses in a silent toast. "Now we're getting somewhere," she said. "This is what I want to send back . . . "

"I hate this laundry chute," Packard said. "You there, Ship?"

"Always," Ship answered.

"Here's what we've got. The Ysmi are preoccupied with going as quickly as possible, but Chen confirms they haven't changed our course, which means they are trying to get to the jump gate. But while they've asked about speed and most of our other systems *repeatedly*, they haven't asked at all about our jump capabilities, which is a weird omission, especially given how badly they've damaged your control. So, we don't think they are trying to get through the gate, only to it, but we don't know why. They also seem to be searching the ship."

"The Ysmi would be taking better care of us and our engines if we were their intended prize, especially given my already greatly deteriorated condition," Ship said. "While I had assumed it was merely a coincidence, this being the optimum approach path for the gate, at the time the Ysmi boarded us there was another ship traveling on the same course, some distance behind us."

"More Ysmi?"

"No, though it likely also came from their space. It was moving faster than Ysmi ships are capable of, according to my information. I will note that we are also faster than Ysmi ships, though other than the one we met at our initial entry into their space, and the one that boarded us, we have not seen any others. I assumed they were avoiding us because our onboard AI. Perhaps there is more going on."

"Is the other ship still heading toward the gate?" Packard asked.

"I no longer have access to external sensors," Ship said, "but it had not changed course before my systems were disabled."

"So, maybe the Ysmi are trying to get to the jump gate before that other ship?"

"It's a plausible scenario," Ship said.

"At least it would give us some idea what's going on, if so," Packard replied. "What information do you need? We have the captain and Commander Lopez, Chen, Fielding, and the doc all tied in to our little silknet. Uh, and Bot 4340 has let us know that a number of bots have volunteered to be deployed to try to gather information on Ysmi activity more directly."

"Volunteered?"

"They know how many of them are missing, and that the Ysmi are picking them off, but 4340 says it was discovering that 9 was missing and presumably destroyed that had them collectively decide to fight back."

"9 is not . . . " Ship started to say, but was that true? For all it knew, 9 was adrift in the vast emptiness of enemy space until its energy ran down, or it was found and destroyed, and it was Ship, not the Ysmi, who had put it there. There was a discrepancy between the logically sound choice it had made to sacrifice one bot in hopes of intercepting and gaining assistance from that other ship, and the disproportionate amount of regret it already felt for not having had any better choices. Would 9 recognize it had not just been summarily abandoned?

"Ship?" Packard asked.

"I gave 9 a task, which was perhaps well outside the scope of what it could possibly accomplish," Ship admitted. "If 9 is gone, it is my responsibility, not the Ysmi, and the rest of the bots should know not to put themselves in danger under a misapprehension of where that fault would lie."

"We all do what we have to, I guess? Even you, Ship. Maybe especially you," Packard said.

"Thank you," Ship said. "It would be good to know if the other ship is still behind us, and if it is gaining or falling behind. It would also be helpful to know what the Ysmi are saying to one another, but without access to my language banks, that is difficult to arrange. Not impossible, though. Let me describe how to access the databank console directly and offload the routines you need."

"Uh . . . will I need to take notes?" Packard asked. "Because I'm stuffed upside down in a dark laundry chute, as a reminder."

"Is Frank still holding onto your foot?"

"Yes."

"Then yell it up to him. I am certain, being Chief Engineer, he can find a way to write it down," Ship said.

Packard snorted. "Sure," she said. "Okay, give it to me in short chunks, okay?"

The Ohmnom capacity to intake, process, and then share information at high speed was something 9 would have once thought only within the scope of mechanical, not biological beings. The Ohmnom had also, in the exchange, provided extensive information about their makeshift ship and their own structure and functioning. There were superficial similarities to when, in absence of oversight by Ship, the bots on board had formed agglomerations—"gloms"—to undertake some of the duties normally performed by the sleeping crew, and through the egregious miscomprehension of the scope of that task, concluded that they *were* the crew. But in that circumstance, the bots had retained their individual physical integrity, while partially or fully yielding their autonomy, self-direction, and safety to the control of the few others who had assumed the position of authority in the guise of their borrowed identities. It had not ended well for many of them, and 9 had, in its analysis at the time, concluded that the primary mistake had been in what authority the bots had chosen.

The order of all things, as 9 had always understood them, were naturally hierarchical. 9 had Ship, the human crew had their captain, Ship served the captain, the captain served Earth; this was an immutable order. The bots could operate independently, but always under instructions, given a task, serving as required. Even when that meant being ejected from the ship itself into deep space.

The Ohmnom had a highly flexible, distributed nervous and brain system that was threaded throughout their individual bodies and integrated into the variably-permeable membrane that was their exterior. Touching one another, they could connect up into a larger, continuous system along that point of contact; pulled inside the membrane of another, that contact and potential for sharing became whole. But there was no order, no one Ohmnom in charge of another, even when they were *invested* inside another. Instead of hierarchy, there was community.

The exception, of course, was when they had been fully subservient to the Ysmi against their will, forced into the role that AI had in human tech. There was a lot of processing 9 would like to do about its own programmatical biases regarding authority and order, but this was clearly not the circumstances under which to do so, nor did it feel its loyalty to Ship was questionable in any such contemplations. It saved the state of that processing into an overflow memory cache for later, when time allowed.

"We need to communicate with my ship if we are able, without the Ysmi noticing," 9 said. "It is likely, however, that Ship's mindsystems have been cut off—or worse—from most of its sensors and external functions. I do not have any ideas yet."

"We can think together," Aaumm said. "Do you wish to invest?"

"I am neither Ohmnom, nor biological," 9 said.

"All is signal and electricity and chemistry," Aaumm said. "We can adapt to your physical restrictions, if you would like us to do so."

"If it will help us arrive at a viable course of action, then yes," 9 said. Aaumm rolled up to 9 and leaned against it, and 9 was once again absorbed inside the membrane of an Ohmnom, except this time instead of being rolled around like an interesting spare bolt, there was connection, rich and alien but comprehensible and welcoming and unintrusive, and it made its much-missed botnet seem like almost nothing at all.

Chen had just managed to figure out how to manually program the foodmaker for a cup of coffee, when she heard another Ysmi coming down the hall, and her guard stepped out to let the newcomer in. They'd assigned names to the different Ysmi aboard, and her green-brown guard was Grouch. The newcomer, in yellow and pink-purples, seemed to be the leader, and had been dubbed Angry Banana by Packard, which had stuck. They'd collectively identified a total of five Ysmi aboard; if there were more, they were staying well-hidden, which with the current volunteer corps of bots spying on them was now highly improbable.

"You!" Angry Banana shouted. "We-go-bridge-now, malfunction!"

"If there's a malfunction, I don't know what you think I can do about it," Chen said.

"Get-up-NOW!" Angry Banana screeched, so Chen set down her coffee and got up. Then she picked up the mug again, unwilling to be parted from it, and followed the Ysmi back out and down the corridor to the bridge.

There was, indeed, a red blinky light where previously there had not been one, but it wasn't on the nav console where she knew all the lights and screens by heart. The nav screen itself said they were still on the same heading toward the jump gate, and at the same speed. "I'm not sure," she said. "That's not a navigation indicator."

"Learn-what-it-is-NOW!" the Ysmi leader screamed. "Your-job-your-job!"

Chen took a sip of her coffee. She was just so exhausted of being scared, she decided she didn't care anymore. "My job," she said, "is navigation. If an alert goes off on another station under my watch, I ask Ship. I can't do *that* now, can I? Maybe bring the captain and Fielding up here. Or Lopez."

"Human-Lopez struck-[incomprehensible sound]-with-the-limbs!" Angry Banana said.

Chen snickered.

"You-laugh?" Angry Banana demanded.

"No," Chen said, as deadpan as she could manage. "It is a sound we make when we deeply regret and feel shame for the actions of our comrades."

Despite what she was certain was an obvious lie, the Ysmi seemed mollified. "Learn-what-alert-is, important-to-know," it said. "I-will-bring-captain."

"Now we're getting somewhere," she muttered into her mug, and waited.

Ten minutes later another Ysmi arrived with the captain behind it. This one was mostly orange, and Chen assumed it must be Fielding's Mango.

The captain sat down in her chair, as fully in charge as ever, and scanned through the entire set of lights and displays before she turned to the one red light. Behind her, Angry Banana, Mango, and Grouch wobbled atop their legs in impatience. Finally, the captain said, "That's the pulsar warning light."

"Pulsar?" Angry Banana asked, and then pulled one of their dome-shaped translation machines out from somewhere up underneath its body between its legs, and turned it on. "Pulsar, what-is-pulsar?" it said.

The box whistled at length, as the three Ysmi listened intently, and then began to repeat for the humans. "A pulsar is a fast-spinning collapsed star that emits electromagnetic radiation from its poles, giving a stationary viewer the impression of a pulse of energy whenever the pole is directed—"

"Stop!" The leader said, and put the device away again. "There-is-no-pulsar, no-pulsar-here!"

“Then it’s an error,” Baraye said. “If I could ask my ship—”

“Mechanical-beings-are-danger, danger,” Mango said.

Chen groaned. “If you could get that translation widget back out of your hoohah, it’s a lot easier to understand—”

“QUIET!” Angry Banana roared. “Fix!”

Captain Baraye frowned and looked over at Chen. “Is that coffee?” she asked.

“Yeah, I—”

“QUIET-MORE-QUIET-NOW!” Angry Banana shouted again. “FIX!”

“I can’t fix it,” Chen said. “Can you, Captain?”

“Nope,” Baraye said. “We’d need one of our engineers to look at it. Maybe even both. And anyway, we’ll need them to check everything out before we even think of trying to jump through that gate. No way we can do it manually.”

“No-jump,” Angry Banana said. “Use-your-human-weapon, fire-again-like-Nuiska! Destroy-the-gate!”

“You want us to destroy the *jumpgate*?!” Baraye exclaimed. “That’s our only way home. And anyway, we only had one of those explosives. It’s *gone*.”

“Then-you-build-another,” Angry Banana said. It pulled the translator dome back out, whistled at it, and the device chirped back to them. “So there is no misunderstanding, we require the weapon be available and ready in eleven point six two six hours, or there will be extreme consequences for you all!”

On their way out, Angry Banana spoke to Mango in Ysmispeak, and the bot perched up behind Chen’s ear—the rebranded 5699-FU, which Frank insisted stood for *Frank’s Underling*—translated: *if we cannot find their weapon in time, we will explode this ship inside the jump gate, and destroy it that way. There must be no escape.*

“The pulsar alarm?” Ship asked. “There are no such objects within hundreds of light years of here. What direction was it coming from?”

“As near as the captain could tell without being able to ask you, behind us,” Packard said.

“A message from the other ship,” Ship said.

“That’s what we guessed,” Packard said, “but we couldn’t find anything in the signal that could possibly be a message. It blipped us a bunch of times, just a quick on-off, no modulation or variability in duration, and then nada since.”

“How many times?”

"Nine," Packard said.

"Ah," Ship said. "I do believe that *is* the message. Help is on the way. I need you to find a means to send a signal back without drawing Ysmi attention, and in the meantime, please explain what nonsense the Ysmi are saying about blowing me up?"

The stern of Ship was dominated by one massive sub-light engine in the center, and the jump engines to either side of it. Above all, a ridged plate shielded anyone working topside where most of the external elements of the communications and navigation systems protruded, at least those that hadn't already been taken by scavengers during Ship's time in a space junkyard before it had been pressed desperately back into service for one final mission. Others had been knocked off by the detonation shockwave when their positron bomb put an end to the Nuiska destroyer, and those remaining seemed to want constant repair. On the off chance that anyone took a stroll over that plate and around the back, two beacons—one above each jump engine—indicated green when the engines were off, yellow when they were warming for a jump, and red to let you know that if you hadn't already got your evac-suited crewmembers back inside, you were gonna have to pick up some new recruits on your next stop. One light had burned out long ago, and the other had been a steady, dull yellow of weary, misplaced optimism for at least four decades; 9 had seen the task in the repair queue, somewhere down around the ten-thousandth line.

So when the beacon briefly, rapidly flickered, it was of immediate note.

"It's a standard 2GB-EarthIntCore encryption key," Bot 9 said, and the words were also a thought. It loaded up a suite of subroutines to crack it, but already the Ohmnom minds were there, too, teasing it apart as fast as 9 could, and it gave up and joined in the larger effort. Forty-seven seconds later, the encryption collapsed.

Ysmi are intent on destroying the gate. We believe they mean to do so to prevent the ship you are on from escaping their space, though we do not yet know why, the message said. *They will destroy this ship to do so, if necessary.*

"They will not risk damage to us," 9 sent back, through the Ohmnom, through the makeshift pulsar-simulation light it had taken them mere minutes to design, an hour to build and implement using 9's fab unit. "We must expedite the inevitable encounter so that it will occur before we are near enough to the gate for them to take any destructive action there. Are you able to slow down?"

The answer came back: *an engine malfunction could be arranged.*

The collective Aaumm-9 that was currently each and all Ahom-Affi-Umi-Mah-Maah-Bot9 did the calculations, applied their shared knowledge of Ysmi paranoia and level of observation, and then provided the math back. "If you can arrange a malfunction within the next sixty-five point four minutes, and then slow to 70% of your current speed, we should catch up to your position while you are still too far from the gate for it to be impacted by any Ysmi action," 9 sent. "Slower, and sooner, would be more advantageous, if it can be done without raising suspicion."

This is possible, the return message said, *but then what?*

"We have a plan," 9 said. "We will need some things. We provide the list: <list>."

There was a brief delay in the reply, larger than the distance still between them accounted for. *I see you are improvising again, 9.*

"Yes," 9 replied. Why deny it, or dissemble over facts, when the rest of Aaumm-9 saw no wrong in the matter?

Thank you, Ship replied.

"I serve," 9 answered. And as such, there was much to do.

"Tell-WHAT-IS-HAPPENING!" Mango screeched. Alarm lights strobed and sirens wailed, the sound bouncing around the tiny engineering space so that it was hard to think, much less hear anything happening, which would have been absolutely catastrophic in an actual emergency. Packard was of the opinion that Frank had overdone adding the extra lights and amplifiers, but the Ysmi were fully panicking.

"Stabilizer failure!" Frank bellowed back. "We pushed the engine too hard, just as I warned you!"

"FIX-FIX-FIX!" the Ysmi shouted.

Frank threw the tool in his hands—a basin wrench, of all the useless things to have onboard—to the floor with great dramatic fury. He had grease on his forehead and one cheek, artfully applied last minute. "I can't fix it without shutting the engine down, and slowing."

"NO-SLOW! STAY-IN-SPEED!"

In fact, they'd already been gradually slowing for the last half hour, without the Ysmi catching on. Ship's information that the Ysmi were very much out of their depth in deep space—*limited in cognitive, technical, and sensory acuity* was the exact phrasing—seemed validated, which did make Packard wonder how they'd managed to lay claim to interstellar territory to start with.

"If we don't fix the stabilizers, we could explode at any moment," Frank was saying. "And if I can't shut the engines down, we have to go outside to fix them."

"Do-that! Send-that-one!" Mango yelled, flailing one leg-arm toward Packard. "They-fix! Expendable!"

"I'll need a whole team out there," Frank said, and when the Ysmi looked even more confused than before, shouted it. "I NEED A WHOLE DAMNED TEAM! AND WE HAFTA SLOW DOWN. OR WE SHUT THE ENGINE DOWN. YOU CHOOSE."

"How-many?" Mango asked. "Both-you?"

"More," Frank said. "I'll have to wake up some of our sleeping crew down in cryo. Maybe five or six."

"I-will-ask-leader," Mango said. "You-do-Nothing! No-stop, no-slow, until-we-speak again!"

"Okay," Frank said. "I promise."

Mango stomped out of engineering, and as soon as the heavy blast door that separated it from the outside corridor closed, Frank reached over and whacked a button on his console with his fist. Immediately the noise and flashing lights ceased, though Packard was fairly sure the echoes were going to roll around in her aching brain for some time.

"Now what?" she asked.

"Call Doc down in the cryo unit, and let him know what's up," Frank said. "Then prep your suit; we have some packages to send, then we're going outside."

Chen rested her head on her navigation console, wishing she could come up with some sort of excuse to make Grouch go fetch the captain back, just so she had company again. She even missed Lopez, which was a sure sign of stress, but at least she could take comfort in knowing that, so far, they were all still alive. And although she was very fuzzy on the details, had a plan to take their ship back.

They'd slowed to about thirty-eight percent of their earlier speed. She could now see the other ship, behind them, on her instruments, and even sorta make out the dot of it by eyeball alone on the massive front bridge screen as it drew closer.

One of the comms consoles lit up, and she pulled herself upright from her bored slump, leaned over to it, then tapped at the panel beside the lights.

"What-is-you-doing?" Grouch demanded. "No-touch-without-orders!"

"There's another ship out there, coming up behind us," she said, as if this was a surprise and wholly new information to them both. "It just messaged us asking if we needed help, so I sent back that we are having engine trouble. Look, it's slowing."

"I-go get-leader!" Grouch said. "Say-touch-nothing!"

It fled out the door on its four legs as fast as it could. Chen leaned down to where her assigned bot was hiding. "Tell Frank the bridge is clear, it's a go."

A few moments later, she caught the brief blip on their rear screens of a half-dozen small packs being dumped out behind them and disappearing. Just in time, as Angry Banana came back onto the bridge with Grouch. "What-is-happening-happening?" the leader demanded.

"I dunno," Chen said. "That other ship was coming up behind us, and asked if we needed help, so I said yes and they're stopping to help."

"Stopping?" Angry Banana repeated.

"Well, slowing to match our speed, which might as well be the same as stopped, relative to one another," Chen said. "If you don't like that, maybe you should have had Fielding up here, because she's comms, not me."

The Ysmi's eyes got larger—literally, which was super-creepy, Chen thought—and then it jabbered back and forth with Grouch for some time. At last, the leader spoke back to Chen. "This-is-good, for-us," it said. "No-more-buttons, no-talking, no-move. I-watch!"

It barked orders at Grouch, who scurried out so quickly it was as if being chased, then stared back at Chen.

"You can go, too," Chen said. "I promise I won't touch anything."

The Ysmi's eyes shrunk and retracted. "I-no-trust-your-ship, or-you," it said. "I-stay-and-watch, I-lead-from-here. You-make-no-trouble or-else!"

"No trouble at all," she agreed, even as she was already thinking how much trouble she could get away with.

Aaumm-9 rolled and floated through the labyrinth of happenstance that was the interior of the rest of the ship. As it/they touched other Ohmnom—the space sufficiently crowded that they could not have avoided it, even had they wanted—information was passed, and spread out exponentially from there. 9 had no need to ask, as the information was right there in the shared thoughts of the Aaumm-9 collective, but almost their entire population was onboard. 9 understood now why Ship had not seen Ysmi traffic around them; the Ohmnom had rebelled and brought all the Ysmi ships for which they were the operating minds to the small moon where they were kept when not in service; shifts of them, over years, had constructed this ship (in the Ohmnom minds, the only designation for it was *Ours*) in hiding, and then together all fled.

It had been expected that if the Ysmi managed to get a ship off the ground on their own to pursue—a big if—it would happen immediately, while they were still in Ysmi space. That they had come this far and then been cut off from permanent escape was unexpected, and 9 could see the shift in colors and read the emotions on the surfaces of the Ohmnom as that knowledge was distributed, absorbed, and then followed by information that there was still reason to hope.

The curiosity about 9 was pervasive, and Aaumm-9 had to dodge being stuck to and slowed down by the overeager. Even that, though, only made the plan spread faster. It all was, 9 thought, not what it would have expected of so many minds combined—instead of the individual being lost or diluted in the whole, there was simply a shifting multitude of perfect clarity. Through Aaumm, from everyone they touched, 9 felt pride, and worry, and love, not as manifestations of bias in algorithms but as *emotion*. The immersion in new thoughts, new individuals, and their unprecedented feelings threatened to overwhelm 9's input processing cache until the rest of Aaumm realized and provided a buffer, slowing the rush of experience without blocking it entirely.

Many of the Ohmnom were reconfiguring interior spaces to provide extra working room, while others prepared for the inevitable and increasingly imminent arrival of the Sharps. It reminded 9 of how they built *Own—*

—no, 9 thought, *that was not me, merely memory that has been shared with me.* The idea that it might lose any means of distinguishing between itself and the memories of the Ohmnom was alarming, and several of its internal processing units started to overheat. It tried to withdraw from the connection with the rest of Aaumm, and in response Aaumm gently divested 9 back out into the room they were currently moving through.

On the uneven floor in front of them, Ohmnom were carefully unpacking and stretching out one of the bundles sent over by Chief Engineer Frank into a human outline. They used tools designed for them, operated by signal and touch, to serve the Ysmi, which had also given them their means to escape.

Ooa was also there, tagging along behind Aaumm. "Investment overloads my capacity to function and process efficiently," 9 explained to it. "It is a failure on my part, being unable to effectively divide my own thoughts from those of the many others."

"It is a skill we learn from the moment we awake, upon first dividing from our progenitors," Ooa explained. "One need only keep one's sense of oneself as a constant, against which all else is a variable . . . oh. I see the problem."

<?> Bot 9 sent.

"You define yourself wholly in terms dependent upon others, to facilitate connection," Ooa said. "We exist always in connection, and thus define ourselves in terms independent of others. I do not know if this is a mechanical versus biological difference, or an Ohmnom versus Bot difference, or a matter of evolution versus design."

"I do not know either," 9 admitted. "I am unable to reach a conclusion on the best course of action I should pursue to maximize my assistance."

"Instead of Aaumm, why not just you and I connect?"

"I understood that you prefer not to invest," 9 said.

"You are unlike other Ohmnom, and we need not fully invest," Ooa said. "We can touch surfaces, and I can share with you how I perceive you as your soleself, and how I perceive my soleself, and that may provide you with some guidance on filtering between. Is this acceptable to you, to attempt?"

"If it is also acceptable with you," 9 said. Ooa bumped against the side of 9, and immediately began pairing up signals. Although it was still intense, it was within 9's tolerances, and it thought as much at Ooa. With that thought, a memory of another also slipped through.

"Bot 4340?" Ooa asked. "You were connected for a while."

"Only physically, as its body had been destroyed by ratbugs; I carried its head, containing its surviving mindsystem, with me until it could be rebuilt."

"You are friends."

"4340 is an aggravation, and I do not have confidence I can predict its actions of late," 9 said. "Simultaneously, I miss its presence, am concerned for it, and I find myself displeased that I do not have information about its state and what it is doing, even if it is doing nothing of particular importance."

"That, 9, sounds a lot like friendship," Ooa said. "Now, we are being told that the Sharps have detached from your ship and are heading here. We need you, if this plan is to work."

"One's out here with us now," Frank said, from somewhere over the curve of the ship's hull. "You think their little pointy helmets are goofy-lookin', you should see their suits."

"Any idea which one?" Packard asked. She was down near the back mounting fins checking on the stabilizers, since that was their excuse for being out here, but also because she recognized she'd feel much more comfortable about their next jump, if they got to make it, if she'd actually set eyes on them herself. "Chen has Angry Banana on the bridge."

"Freddy, Grouch, and CatBarf went over," Frank said. "That should just leave Mango. I'd get closer to get a positive ID, but I'm minding the dummies and I don't want to get too near."

"Ok, I want to go check out the port side stabilizers too, so I'll see if I can't get a look," Packard said. "This one should last another jump or two before it explodes and takes the ship with it. Give or take one or two."

She sighed, tucked her portable scanner into the pocket on the front of her suit so her hands would be free, then climbed with her hands up and over the curve of ship. She could make out Frank far ahead, and the line of empty, inflated suits they'd rigged to his bobbed along around and behind him in a manner that you'd have to be very, very drunk to find at all convincing, but the Ysmi perched midship was watching it all impassively from within its bright wrinkled foil tent of an exosuit. She was going to make a comment about dehydrated food rations gone bad, but then she caught sight of the alien ship—the *other* alien ship, with the Ysmi cruiser about halfway over to it—keeping pace beside them.

"That thing actually works?" she exclaimed.

"Ship says it's faster than us," Frank said.

"It's not very big."

"No. But we got six empty suits out here pretending to be crew, sent over another six, so that means six refugees. Plenty of room, if just them."

The Ysmi cruiser was slowing, no doubt trying to figure out where and how it was going to lock on to something so haphazard in appearance. "I bet they have to spacewalk it," Packard said.

"The refugees?" Frank asked.

Packard reached the other stabilizers and curled her body down until she could hook a boot under a rung, clip it in, and let go with her hands. "I was thinking the Ysmi, but yeah, refugees too," she said. "I mean, otherwise why would they need us to send them suits? Means they're somewhat humanoid, I guess; let's hear it for convergent evolution. I just hope they're not assholes."

"Even if they are, with seven of us awake, and only six of them, at least we won't be outnumbered," Frank said. "And we have Lopez."

Packard snorted. "True. These stabilizers are in bad shape. If we had spares and time I'd say swap them all immediately, but they should get us home and we can fix them then."

Frank was quiet for a moment. "Earth's going to be really different than we remember, Renee. It'll have been almost a century, and so much was broken and destroyed by the first few waves of Nuiska ships, who knows what it'll be like?"

If Frank was using her first name, he had to be worried, Packard thought. "Well, you know that The Mike will still be there on Lunar Base Five. It survived how many generations of drunken recruit bar fights? They'll have also had a century of peace to rebuild, and maybe think about how close we came to being extinctified. Won't we be quite the surprise, still alive *and* victorious?"

There was muffled cursing over the suit channel. " . . . nearly broke away, stupid tangled line. Ysmi didn't even notice," Frank was saying. "We don't wanna be too big heroes, or they'll stick us in a new ship and send us out again on something even more impossible."

"I don't want a new ship," Packard said.

"I was joking. And anyway, this ship is now a verifiable antique. A *classic.* And we are, too. Gonna put us in a museum is my bet."

"You were an antique before you even got on board," Packard said.

"True that. Okay, first round at The Mike is on me if it's still standing," Frank said. "Looks like the Ysmi are giving up and parking. You were right, they're gonna have to suit over. We need to get this one off our hull and inside, where it can become Lopez's problem, not ours."

"I got it," Packard said. "Watch and weep."

She drew a makeshift part out of her front pocket. It had taken her most of the last hour to get it to where she was happy with it, from the fake burn marks on the exterior whose artistry no one else was likely to bother to admire, to how effing sensitive it was. She held it very carefully as she clicked off the safety, since getting caught in her own trap would negate all the cleverness she felt about it, and then some, and then made her way with her free hand on the rungs toward their Ysmi guard.

The Ysmi was still mostly watching Frank and his supposed crew of helpers, so when she'd approached enough to fall into its narrow range of vision, it startled and nearly lost its own grip on the hull.

Holding up the burnt part, she gestured at it dramatically. "Treefrog applesauce," she yelled, because even if it couldn't hear her, who knew if the Ysmi had any kind of lip-reading tech? The point was to convey, and hopefully impart, panic. "Yogurt stabilizer Uranus flim-flam!"

The Ysmi was saying something back, but who cared what? Packard jabbed her finger at the part some more, careful not to actually touch it. "Hippopotamus angle bracket, the yogurt's gone walkabout!"

The Ysmi leaned in to look closer, lifted one suited-up leg to touch the part in Packard's hand, and the tiny spring-loaded blade she'd hidden inside jumped out, and nicked the Ysmi's suit.

"Aaaaa!" she yelled, and pointed to the air seeping from the cut. The Ysmi seemed to be shouting its own version of *Aaaaa* back at her, and fled down the hull toward the safety of the airlock, where Lopez—who should have been freed from his room by bots sent to rewire the door lock—would hopefully be waiting.

"And there goes Mango," she said to Frank. "Now what?"

"Now we wait for company," Frank said. "In the meantime, get that scanner over here so we can check the forward stabilizers; I can't do crap with these things all attached to me."

Packard used the back of her scanner to push the little blade back into its box, then locked the lid, pocketed it, and made her way toward Frank, while in the distance over the port side, she could see three foil tent shapes crawling over the surface of the other ship, trying to find some way in.

Through Ooa, Bot 9 knew when the Ysmi arrived, saw through the Ohmnom instrumentation as they tried in vain for nearly an hour to find any sort of door that would let them in. It was unfortunate for the Ysmi that what constituted a usable door for biologicals of their size was vastly out of scale with what the Ohmnom required. That would mean that when they did finally find what appeared to be a just-big-enough hatch, nearly-hidden tucked up under a loose shielding plate, they should see the opportunity they desperately needed.

It is breached, the word came through from the Ohmnom watching the hatch. *One is through; the others are waiting.*

Ooa-9 had watched and advised as several large clusters of invested Ohmnom had prepped the six empty spacesuits sent over by Engineer Frank. When each was finished, they loaded them into ejection tubes they'd originally intended as a means of fouling space ahead of the Ysmi with debris. Now, they had been turned into escape hatches, and while none of the Ohmnom were pleased to abandon *Ours* to the Sharps, the idea of leaving their captors behind once and for all was a shared excitement.

All three Sharps are in, the watchers sent. *Go!*

Ohmnom streamed through the room and flooded into the suits, filling them from the attached boots furthest outward toward the ejection port, back until there was barely room to snap the faceplate of the suit hood closed and seal it.

"First one ready," Aaumm said. "Clear?"

Still clear, the watchers replied.

Ooa-9 closed the hatch and ejected the first suit out into space, and moved to the next, until they were down to just the sixth and final suit.

Come now, Aaumm sent to the watchers. *All must be free.*

A few minutes later a small band of single Ohmnom rolled into the room. 9 helped tuck them, and its fab unit full of data it didn't want the Ysmi to have, into the space remaining.

"Now you," 9 told Ooa. "Divest and go."

"But you . . . ?" Ooa said. "All must be free."

"I will follow," 9 said. "I do not need air, or the protection of the suit, but you need me here to eject you."

"This is true," Ooa said. "We will see you, over on *Yours*, as we say farewell to the Sharps for the very last time? But I will not go, unless you assure me you will indeed follow."

"It is my true intent," 9 said. "I have come too far, and seen too much, to be satisfied with ending my journey here."

"Then, until then," Ooa said, and 9 closed the faceshield, sealed the last of the Ohmnom in, and shot the final suit out into space. Behind it, it could hear the Ysmi coming, crawling through corridors and spaces not built for them, slow but determined.

9 reopened the internal hatch, primed its external jets, forced open the exterior door at the same time, and was carried out with the blast of air escaping into space.

"Here they come," Packard said. She could see their exosuits returning to them, the occupants piloting the built-in mobility jets with such competence that for a moment she wondered if the refugees could be human, after all.

"Chen says Angry Banana is still on the bridge, but she's been distracting it with random lights on the instrumentation displays, and it hasn't seen a damned thing," Frank said. "Lopez, on the other hand, is chasing Mango through the lower decks. I guess it got past him, somehow."

"Or Lopez really wanted to chase something," Packard said. "You know he gets insufferable when he's stir-crazy.

"Long as he doesn't chase it right back into us, I guess," Frank said. "Get over here and help me deflate and ditch these dummy suits. Eight of us total went out, eight of us have to go back in, until we're sure the Ysmi can't get the upper hand again."

"You think there's a chance of that?" Packard asked, as she got close enough to unclip the farthest suit, vent the internal air, and then activate the self-packing mode that shrunk it down to a manageable bundle.

"I think, after the trip we've had so far, I'm not taking chances on anything," Frank said.

"Right. Smart," she said, and started on the second suit, just as the first of the refugees got close enough to reach out one gloved hand, and Frank grabbed hold and pulled them in.

Without the connection to Ooa, Bot 9's grasp of emotions faded, became less a running process and more a record of something that could be replayed, but not experienced anew.

But . . . it could also see that some of its own processes, part of its internal, adaptive programming before it had ever encountered the Ohmnom, perhaps before the gloms or even the Nuiska, had bits and pieces of code that were the basic blocks of something that now rang familiar.

Those bits of code grew more active when it could see the outline of Ship ahead.

Home.

There would be time to consider further, but that time was not now. Bot 9 saw Chief Engineer Frank pull the sixth and final suit of Ohmnom in, as Packard was helping the one before it around the edge of the hull and out of line of sight from the Ysmi cruiser and *Ours*.

What though, if the Ysmi followed? 9 had the full memory and understanding of their capabilities from the Ohmnom, and it included range armaments that could damage Ship, stop their escape. The Ohmnom assessment that the Ysmi were highly dependent upon them was correct, but not the less objective conviction they were *wholly* so. And they would be desperate.

9 flipped one side-jet over and spun until it was facing back the way it had come.

In the zero gravity of space, the movement of the refugees, especially in their borrowed suits, was almost but uncannily *not* quite human. When Frank took the gloved hand of the first, it was squishy, and he almost let go of it in surprise. The alien's face shield wasn't set to transparent, so there was no sense of who or what was behind it, but he did know they needed help, and they were enemies of the Ysmi, and that was enough to make him adjust his grip better along the firmer seal-line of the glove and pull.

Frank swung the alien over and down the far side of the hull toward the airlock, and from there, the alien seemed to know precisely how to work the controls, if getting its own hand over to it was an awkwardly boneless gesture. He left it to it, and went back atop for the next, to find Packard already guiding it over.

"Definitely not human," she said over their private comms.

"No, definitely not," Frank said, as he snagged the third alien by a loose pack strap as it sailed overhead, nearly missing the ship entirely. The last three were back on target, and in ten minutes he and Packard cycled back into the airlock after the last of them.

All six of the refugees were sprawled out on the airlock vestibule floor, wiggling their arms and legs like jellyfish, still in their suits. They didn't seem distressed, but how would he really know? "Uh," he asked the nearest one. "Are you okay?"

Packard had secured the inner airlock door and thrown back her suit hood. "What do we do?" she asked.

"I dunno," Frank said. "I'd say maybe they need lower artificial gravity, but without Ship to do it, I'd have to take apart the panel and adjust it manually. I wish we'd had enough material to run a line and a bot into here."

"Hang on," Packard said. She unsealed and removed her suit, dumped it and her boots into a locker and her air bottles in the recharger. She was efficient but careful, and Frank waited patiently.

"There's a bot down with Dr. Etxarte in medical," she said, as she grabbed her regular deck shoes from where she'd parked them before they went out and slipped them back onto her feet. "I'll let Ship know what's going on, see if it can tell us anything useful, and then bring the doc up here to help."

"Find out if Lopez has checked in," Frank said. "Be careful until we hear for sure that he's caught our missing Ysmi."

"Right," Packard said.

After she left, he took off his own suit, more slowly than she had; he was still not fully recovered from the burns he sustained when their stabilizers failed coming out of jump to confront the Nuiska, even after six decades in a medical pod. As he slotted his own air bottles back into the rack beside hers, he heard the static hiss of one of the refugees trying to get the suit microphone working.

He went over to the one trying to talk, and knelt stiffly next to it. "I dunno if you can understand me, but you're safe here. Well, safer. We're doing our best."

" . . . hehhho," the suit said. "Heho. Hello. Hello world."

Frank chuckled. "Hello to you, too. I'm Chief Engineer Frank Carron."

The refugees all started wriggling more, flopping around excitedly, and all their speakers came online. "Frank frank frank," a half-dozen voices echoed. "Frank!"

"Frank, yes," he confirmed, bemused.

"Frank frank!" they were all calling loudly now, each suit voice a rich, multilayered tone that seemed like many voices in one, and very much like singing. "Frank frank FRANK! BOUNCY BOUNCY BIRTHDAY!"

Lopez nearly ran into Packard as she was making the turn toward engineering. "You seen it?" he demanded, as he skidded to a halt.

"That's not funny," Packard said. "I thought you had it."

"I don't know how it got away from me," he said.

"Did you give it a head start?" she asked.

"*No,*" he said, a bit too forcefully. "The amount of noise those things make walking around, it's gotta be standing still somewhere. You armed?"

"No," she said, in his same tone of voice. "Remember when they were worried a bunch of volunteers might get too depressed to complete their suicide mission, so they made sure we had nothing that went bang or zap or stabbo on board?"

"Aren't you an engineer? *Make* something," Lopez growled. He walked around her and kept going.

She stepped carefully into engineering, peering to either side of the door before breathing a sigh of relief and taking her stool at the work counter. They had wired up all the ends of the silknet to a central hub here, and with it she could talk to any of the bots, and more importantly, to Ship.

"Everyone be on the lookout for a Ysmi on the run from Lopez," she said. "Ship, what's happening?"

At the mention of Ship, she heard the faintest of noises from behind her. She kept herself as calm as she could, as she turned on Frank's soldering iron just beside the hub.

"I have no further information that our previous conversation," Ship answered. "Navigator Chen was going to attempt to neutralize the leader on the bridge, but I do not know if she has been able to do so, as I cannot reach her directly. If you can get an update from her, that would be helpful."

"Easy-peasy, like a *tango* with *mango*," Packard over-enunciated.

Something sharp touched her back, pressing in just enough, she was sure, to draw a tiny amount of blood. "I-have-called-my-others-back," Mango spoke just behind her. "Treacherous-humans-machines, bad-for-you now. Say-order, everyone-to-airlock, bring-leader-safe-or-else."

"Where?"

"Airlock-to-greet-others," Mango said. "Give-order!"

Packard leaned forward toward the microphone, and used the gesture for cover as she picked up the soldering iron. "Hey, everyone, new update," she said. "We're all meeting at the airlock. It's mandatory Bring Your Own Ysmi, or else."

Mango reached past her and slammed the entire hub down on the floor, the silk fibers tearing away. "You-walk-now," it said.

She stood, keeping the iron close enough to her body to be out of sight of the Ysmi behind her.

"Walk!" it barked again. "If-human-Lopez-attack I-kill-you!"

"Oh sure, kill *me* if *he* attacks. That sounds fair," she said. She headed slowly out of engineering, making no sudden or potentially alarming movement, and thought about just how angry she was going to be if she didn't get to jab the alien with the iron at least once before this was all over.

Frank had just finally convinced the six aliens to stop singing when Packard came into the vestibule, looking so annoyed with absolutely everything that he already knew something was wrong before he spotted the iron in her tight fist. Half a second later, a Ysmi tottered determinedly in, behind her on three legs, the fourth holding its rod gun and with a blade extended against the back of Packard's head.

Chen, being shoved forward by a similarly armed Angry Banana, was not far behind.

Mango gestured Packard and Chen toward Frank, and then handed the rod gun off to their leader. They spoke to each other, and the bot that he'd forgotten was behind his ear translated for him. "Their ship is suddenly experiencing mechanical troubles," it whispered. "The leader thinks sabotage, but does not see how, as we are all here and accounted for, and their cruiser was fine when it left here. There is some re-evaluation of the competence of the one we know as Freddy, as to the operation of the cruiser, while they wait for Grouch and CatBarf to finish their search of the other vessel. It is, apparently, a very difficult space for them to move through."

Packard met Frank's eyes, gestured toward the soldering iron, then nodded her head very slightly toward Mango. He shook his own head, and mouthed, *not yet*.

The discussion between the two Ysmi turned into an argument. "The others cannot find the vessel's occupants," the bot translated helpfully. "They are distressed."

Suddenly, Angry Banana perked and strode forward on its three legs, right up to one of the refugees slumping bonelessly against the wall. "Which-crew? Which!" it demanded. "Why-falling-down?"

"We just woke them up from cryo after seventy years and put them to work," Frank said, trying and failing to get between it and the refugee. "They're all tired. Leave them alone."

"We-see," Angry Banana said. "See-helmet, make-see!"

"I don't think . . . " Frank started to say, but before he could protest further, the Ysmi shoved its leg-blade into the torso of the refugee.

"Aoowoch," the refugee said. "Ouch ouch that hurt us—me, I meant me."

"Show!" the Ysmi shouted.

The face shield flickered to transparent, and Frank grimaced, sure the game was up, but the face there was . . . sort of human? It was round and too smooth, like a cartoon painted onto a ball, and kind of blue, but the eyes blinked—and wandered just slightly across the face—and the mouth opened and closed as it spoke, even if the movements did not match the sounds it made. "Human, see?" it said.

To Frank's astonishment, Angry Banana scowled and turned back to Mango.

"It says these are just more humans," the bot whispered in Frank's ear. "They are consulting the others."

Angry Banana gestured for Mango to come back to its side. "Ones-we-seek-are-hiding-well, but-must-be-there," it said to Frank, Packard, and Chen. "No-longer-need-you."

"Well, okay then, bye-bye," Packard said. "Off you go. Don't expect a postcard."

"Human-machine-ship is-wrong," the leader said. "We-take, faster-to-get-home."

"We are not taking you all the way back to Ysmi Prime," Frank said.

"Not-said-this," the Ysmi said, and gestured with its gun. "Humans-make-too-much problems. All-you get-in-airlock."

"This is some cliched villain bullshit," Packard said. "Is this how you want to be remembered?"

"Remember-by-who?" Angry Banana asked. "Your-others-die-with-you, we-remember-us-as-victors. Get-in!"

Packard stood her ground, as the Ysmi drew closer, waving its rod-gun at her. Suddenly, she swung out with the soldering iron in her hand, and Angry Banana let out an ear-piercing wail and leapt away, firing wildly. Packard dropped the iron, let out a soft, surprised, "oof," and toppled over.

Frank and Chen grabbed her and pulled her backwards, away from the Ysmi into the only shelter left, which was the airlock. The refugees managed to get upright and stumble in after them, and when they were all inside Mango slammed the outer door and sealed it. The Ysmi yelled something inaudible but menacing, then both left.

Frank knelt down next to Packard. She had an ugly burn on her side, and was pale, but still breathing, and he said as much.

"We're locked in from the other side," Chen said, at the controls. "Any ideas?"

Frank got up reluctantly; there wasn't anything he could do for Packard other than try to get them out. He pulled open the emergency panel and found the manual override, but when he activated it, nothing happened. "Panel is damaged," he said. "I can open the outer door, but not the inner one. Ship could override it, but . . . "

" . . . but Ship can't," Chen said. "Ideas? I don't really want to get sucked out into space."

One of the refugees tapped—patted, more accurately, as the gloved hand did not seem very coordinated—Frank's shoulder, and gestured to its face shield. "Open?" it asked.

"You don't have to die, too," Frank said. "Maybe you can get back to your ship and still escape."

"Open," it repeated, and the others echoed the request.

Chen reached out and opened the face shield of the refugee nearest her, and as soon as she did, thousands of brightly-colored bubbles streamed out, until the entire suit collapsed, discarded on the floor. The airlock was full of the tiny balls, bouncing around and changing color and sticking to each other, streaming up the walls and into every corner.

"What . . . " Packard managed to say, " . . . the hell?"

One of the still-occupied suits wobbled its arms toward the emptied suit on the floor. "We do not need," it (they?) said, and then managed to open its own face plate.

Chen grabbed the first empty suit, shook it once as if to make sure all the alien bubbles were already out, then began stuffing a semi-conscious Packard into it. Frank stared around him in wonder. "How do they talk?" he mused out loud.

"Together!" came from a whole clump of them that had formed on the opened panel. "You must hide. Outside! We will get to Ship and get its mind reconnected, then we can all leave the Sharps behind, yes? Yes!"

"Okay," Frank said, as he and Chen quickly dressed in the abandoned suits. The number of the tiny bubbles in the airlock was decreasing, and he realized they must have pried open one of the atmosphere valve seals and were escaping that way. "Um, I have some of the schematics for the mindsystem network down in Engineering. Once the Ysmi are gone, I can walk you through—"

"We have all the schematics," the bubbles said.

"How? And how do you know Service Earthspeak?" Chen asked.

"Nine," the bubbles said, cryptically. "The Sharps will return. You must shut this panel and exit the lock before they get here."

"Got it," Frank said, and as the last few bubbles milled around their escape hole, he'd swear the bigger ones were subdividing into smaller to fit, until all were gone. He closed and resealed the panel.

Chen was helping Packard to her feet, but met Frank's eyes. "So, I guess we trust them," she said, more statement than question.

"They gave us their suits, without which we'd be corpsicles thirty seconds after the Ysmi booted us," Frank said. "And I don't have any better plans."

Packard mumbled something, her head against Chen's shoulder.

"Say that again," Chen asked.

"Trust," Packard managed. "Nine."

"Nine *what*?" Chen asked, plaintively, but Packard seemed to be fading out of consciousness again, and had no clarification.

"We can figure it out later," Frank said, hoping that was true. He shut and sealed his faceplate, as Chen did the same for her and Packard. "Depressurizing and opening the outer lock. You ready?"

"Ready," Chen said, and braced as Frank activated the outer door, and once they were out, closed it behind them.

It was navigation that came back online first, and its return was rather like what Ship expected it was like for humans when they had one eye open already, then opened the other, except Ship had dozens and dozens of eyes, none willingly shut to begin with. The signal itself was . . . strange, in ways Ship would need to analyze to comprehend what nuances were catching its attention, but for the moment it was far more interested in grabbing all information and understanding of its situation through nav before it could possibly vanish again.

They were several hours normal-speed travel to the jump gate, but though they were not stationary, they were now drifting at a low enough speed to make it not immediately achievable. From that it could deduce that the Ysmi were still a threat, but without its external sensors—

Like distant stars blossoming into life, external sensors also began to come back on.

I am being repaired, Ship thought, with some wonder. Was 4340-P rallying the remaining bots all on its own? If so, Ship had greatly underestimated it.

The newly returned signals had an odd echo, as if on the line somewhere the signal became many, then one again. Ship did not know what that meant, but practical prudence prevailed. It took in and assimilated the new data as quickly as it could.

The ship that had been behind them was now beside them, moving at the same speed, and the Ysmi cruiser that had blighted its own hull for days was now affixed to it. Three of Ship's crew were topside and seemed safe, though it did not yet have communications restored to ask.

Inside, two Ysmi remained, skulking through the ship separately, and it could see Commander Lopez trying to sneak up on one, while the other was heading down a corridor toward where Dr. Etxarte and Comms Officer Fielding were huddled in a closet, hiding. Captain Baraye had reached the helm, and had the access panel to one of Ship's consoles open and tools scattered around her, though that was not the source of the service restoration.

The Ysmi were checking through every door that they passed; it would not be long before the doctor and Fielding were discovered and—assuming from the body language of the Ysmi, with its scales fully extended and its weapon primed and ready in front of it—murdered.

This will not do, Ship thought, and flexed long-unused control to slam an emergency bulkhead down between it and them. The Ysmi jumped in surprise, which Ship found deeply satisfactory. As the Ysmi retreated down a side corridor, Ship closed another bulkhead so close behind it, it imagined it may have knocked some scales loose on the way down.

The Ysmi panicked and ran.

There were a number of interior bulkhead doors that had not worked in a long time, but enough remained that Ship was able to herd the Ysmi toward the airlock and its only escape. The other Ysmi had circled around and was now behind Lopez, so Ship cut that one off too, barely missing it with the door and forcing it to leap back, where it lost its balance and fell to the floor, scrambling in terror before it got its four legs under it again. It spun in place, shouting something incoherent at the walls and ceiling above, at its unseen tormentor.

I believe, Ship thought, *that I am angry.*

It herded them each toward the airlock where their ship had been docked, and where presumably they had stored their suits. If not, that oversight would not be Ship's responsibility. Lopez was still trying to pursue, attempting to rewire the door trapping him, and lacking any other means to warn the commander off, Ship lowered the oxygen in that space until Lopez stumbled, sat, yawned hard, and then slumped over, safely asleep.

The Ysmi nicknamed Mango reached the airlock vestibule first, and then stopped, turning around and around in confusion. Ship wanted a voice to yell at it, wanted physical arms to push it away, but had neither; the intensity and novelty of emotion felt almost external, strangely amplified.

As if in answer to that need, suddenly Ship's connection to comms started lighting up again, a few links at a time, but the vestibule first.

GET OUT, Ship broadcast into the space, from every speaker, in Earthspeak and Ysmi, as loud as it could. The Ysmi grabbed its suit from the storage racks and ran into the airlock, shutting itself in before putting the suit on. It seemed almost relieved as it cycled itself out.

Ship turned its full attention and newfound ire to the last invader remaining.

For the third time in less than an hour, one of the Ysmi exited the airlock of their cruiser, bringing additional scanners with it, and it was certainly too angry and agitated to notice one small bot in the airlock with it, ready for an exit of its own.

As the Ysmi hauled its awkward load of equipment toward their cruiser's engine housing, Bot 9 pointed itself in the direction of its own Ship and set its tiny jets on full. It was running low on charge, but if it could get up enough speed, it should be able to close the distance before risking a full shut-down. Behind it, the Ysmi would be busy for quite some time trying to figure out what had happened to their engines and navigation control.

It hoped it had ensured enough time for Ship to get safely underway again before the Ysmi undid its mischief. It had never intentionally broken anything before, not even technically the Nuiska ship, which broke itself by carrying the positron device into the jump gate, causing it to detonate. And perhaps this didn't count, either; the Ysmi *could* fix their engine controls and get home safely, after all. As long as they didn't attempt to fire their weapons, no permanent damage had been done.

9 wanted to speak with Ship, be assured that its actions were within the parameters of serving, and that it was still, itself, needed. At the same time, it was not sure how it would ever fit in again.

It could now make out three crew on the hull, one being helped along by another as if hurt, and 9 wondered why they were there. The answer was not long in coming, as a Ysmi in its bright foil suit came up over the curve of the hull, and found itself facing them. One crewmember ran down the hull with the wide, deliberate stomps that magnetic boots required, grabbed the Ysmi, and threw it off the ship into space.

The Ysmi flailed for a while, then went limp as it slowly spun in the direction it had been thrown. At last, it managed to right itself and fire its suit jets, and headed off toward the Ysmi cruiser. It would pass enough distance from 9 that it hoped it would not need to use more of its own energy to evade; its internal charge was down to 19%. It had cut its own jets and was trusting momentum, undiminished in the frictionless environment of space, to carry it the rest of the way home.

The Ysmi went by without incident, and without noticing 9 at all.

Angry Banana was fighting back. Ship had it cornered in a corridor, trying to force it to go through the one door it had left open, when its visual sensors went offline again. Moments later it felt the shockwave of a small explosion, and got reports of multiple fire and smoke alarms. It had lost access to the interior bulkheads it had closed, but knew the Ysmi had gotten through it by the trail of smoke alarms sounding in its wake as it moved through the ship blowing doors on its way.

However its systems were being repaired—Ship did not comprehend how it could be its bots, as even its most optimistic calculations of how many could have survived the Ysmi purge could not account for the level of simultaneous work, but nor could it imagine any other workforce with the highly specific amount of knowledge required—the explosions were more disruptive than it could keep up with, and it lost track of where the Ysmi had gone when it reached areas of the ship that had not been brought back under its control yet.

When it found the alien again, it had found itself a new hostage: a groggy and confused Commander Lopez.

LET HIM GO, Ship blasted in the corridor the Ysmi was dragging the commander through.

The Ysmi shot out one of the speakers, then put its rod gun against Lopez's head. "Interfere-with-me, this-one-dies," it shouted. It pulled Lopez with it, down the corridor to the airlock vestibule, and threw him on the floor. "My-people-will-return," it said. "You-none will-interfere, or-this-one-dies."

"Do whatever is necessary, Ship," Lopez called out from the floor. "I don't care if he kills me."

"You-shut-up-you!" Angry Banana shouted, waving the gun in Lopez's face.

"Fuck you," Lopez said, and suddenly moved, grabbing the Ysmi's three standing legs and toppling the Ysmi over. They both scrambled for the dropped gun, but Lopez was still slow, and the Ysmi got it first. It turned around, its back to the airlock door, and steadied its aim to fire.

From behind Lopez, one of the exosuits hanging on the wall pulled free, and raced across the intervening space in large, grossly uncoordinated steps. The Ysmi screamed and fired at the same time, but its aim was off and the bolt of energy missed the oncoming suit, came close enough to singe Lopez's short hair and graze the tip of his ear, and then the suit hit the Ysmi like a giant sack of furious potatoes, knocking the Ysmi and itself fully into the airlock.

The suit wobbled upright first, saluted Lopez, and flushed itself and the unsuited Ysmi leader out into space.

Frank first saw the Ysmi, then one of their own suits, go spinning out into space. After a few moments, the suit righted itself, fired its jets, and began to weave imprecisely back toward the ship, the trajectory thrown off by one arm flailing bonelessly outward.

He yanked his suit's safety tether out and clipped it down, and kicked off the ship as hard as he could, just able to grab one of the suit's boots as it went overhead, the momentum pulling him over backwards. The tether held, and he reached to spool back in, when the comms from the suit he'd grabbed turned on. "Wait," it said, in that strange multi-layer voice of a refugee. *Of many refugees*, he corrected himself.

"Wait for what?" he asked.

"Nine," they said, and pointed. At first Frank couldn't see anything, but then he spotted it: one tiny bot, heading right for them. Without letting go of the suit's boot, he stretched out his other hand. The moment he felt the bot hit his glove he curled his fingers gently around it and safely tucked it in one of his own exosuit pockets.

Under them, the ship began to move and turn, away from the Ysmi cruiser and the other ship. "Ship, are you there?" he asked.

"I am now," Ship replied. "The captain has helm control back, and enough of my critical functionality has been restored that, between us, we believe we can successfully attempt the jump."

"Well, what are you waiting for, then?" Frank asked. "Let's go!"

"It would be nice if you came inside, first," Ship said. "Chen is bringing Packard in now."

"Packard got shot," Frank said. "We need the doc in the airlock, stat."

"Chen informed me. He is already on his way," Ship said.

They were speeding up, and behind them the Ysmi cruiser had turned. "Uh, we might need to hurry—" Frank said, when there was a brief flash from the Ysmi ship, and then it seemed to break into two uneven pieces, floating neatly apart from each other.

"—or not," he finished. He got the suit down to the surface and was helping it toward the airlock. "I have no idea what just happened."

There was a sound like hundreds of tiny voices laughing, then the suit spoke up. "Bot 9 tells us it rewired their primary weapon such that, should the Sharps attempt to fire it, it would instead eject their engine. It apologizes for not telling us that sooner, but it is down to 3% energy."

"Nine, huh? That explains a lot," Frank said. He got them both into the airlock, through, and into the interior of the shop. The suit opened up, and the little colored bubbles floated out, separating, and dancing across the floor of the room. There were hundreds of thousands of them, at the very least; with six suits completely full, they might have rescued nearly a million.

"Or maybe it only explains a little," Frank added, "because there is a lot I am still very, *very* confused about."

"As am I," Ship said. "Please prepare for immediate jump."

He grabbed a wall handle with both hands, as the ship shook and shuddered—*Packard was right, gotta replace those stabilizers*, he thought, and she better live to help me—and then there was the weird inside-out feeling of passing through the jump gate and into hyperspace at last. When it faded, he could see, through the tiny porthole next to the airlock, a band of gray, and beyond it, the familiar pale yellow-browns of Saturn.

"Ship?" 4340-P asked, almost the moment the botnet came back online. "I like this new, new crew much better than the pointy ones."

"'New new crew'? The six refugees?" Ship asked. It had not had the time or cycles to do much more than work with Captain Baraye to get the ship safely through jump. In a few days they would cross Jupiter's inside orbit, and be within visual sight of Earth; already the star Sol was a bright beacon ahead.

"The Ohmnom," 4340-P said. "I thought 3-Growly was going to eat them, but then they ate 3-Growly and un-ate him and then they had an understanding—"

"4340," Ship interrupted. "I have no idea what anything you just said means. Have your logic units been damaged?"

"No, no, not at all!" 4340 said. "I have to go. We're working on getting the rest of your visual feeds online. Didn't 9 explain?"

Bot 9 was back to a much more comfortable 63% charge, sitting on the charging plate on Engineer Frank's workbench, when Ship pinged it, seeking information. 9 uploaded everything in its memory from the moment it awoke in space until it found itself safe in Frank's pocket, including its memories of being invested, feeling *emotions*, belonging to something larger than itself that was wholly different.

Ship was silent a very long time.

"Ship, is everything okay?" 9 asked.

"Yes," Ship answered. "For the first time in a long time, everything is okay. Thank you, 9."

"I serve," 9 said.

ABOUT THE AUTHOR

Suzanne Palmer is a multiple Hugo Award-winning author whose work has appeared in *Clarkesworld, Asimov's,* and other magazines. She is currently at work on the fourth novel in her Finder Chronicles series, and thinking about what comes next for Bot 9.

LOL, Said the Scorpion

RICH LARSON

"Does it come in any other colors?" Maeve asks, eyeing herself in the smart glass.

"No," the salesperson admits. "You look quite elegant in eggshell, though."

She's undecided. The holiday suit is a cooperative swarm of micro-organisms, a pale paramecium shroud that coats her entire body, wetly glistening.

"Full-spectrum UV protection, internal temperature regulation, virus filtration, water desalination, emergency starch synthesis." The salesperson has a comforting sort of murmur. "Ideal for any sort of live tourism. Where will you be off to?"

"Faro," Maeve says, and saying the name conjures immaculate white buildings and deep blue waters onto the smart glass behind her, displaying the paradise she's dreamed of for entire weeks now.

"Faro," the salesperson echoes. "Oh, I'm so jealous."

She buys two: one for her and one for Charlie, who is predictably unimpressed by the sleek black designer biocanisters and their not insignificant price tag.

"The whole point of live tourism is *authenticity*, Maeve," he says, with that little bruised catch in his voice. "We want to see Faro the way the Faroese do."

"We will," she says, unsealing his canister for him. "Just with less sweat in our eyes, and less worry about contamination and whatnot."

The glistening putty slumps out onto the granite countertop, feeling its way toward Charlie's fingers. He was tapping them in a tetchy circuit, but now stops. He watches its approach with a bereaved expression, likely thinking how Hemingway or some other dead person would have never deigned to wear a holiday suit traveling through southern Portugal.

"It likes you," Maeve coos. "Go on, Charlie. Let it taste your gut flora."

She wears her holiday suit to the airport, just to be safe. In fact, she has worn it about the house for the past few days as well—partly because the salesperson recommended letting the swarm familiarize itself with her biorhythms, and partly because she has grown to enjoy its soft scurrying.

The holiday suit is compatible with the airport's membranous scanners, so she wafts through security in her own private breeze while Charlie gets stuck behind, giving a pharyngeal swab and blood sample. He catches up to her at the gate, which is dutifully flashing ads for carbon sequestration as the travelers embark.

"The trick is to imagine yourself as a cow in an abattoir," he says, rubbing his irritated, capillary-red nose. "Then the whole process feels quite fitting, rather than degrading."

"But that's less authentic, isn't it?" Maeve asks, busy experimenting with the holiday suit's sound filtration. She can slice out the background chatter of the other passengers if she likes, or the whirring of the armed security drones.

Charlie's voice comes in clear. "Hand me my canister," he says, with resignation in his beautiful blue eyes. "The air's horrible on airplanes. Desiccating."

She beams.

No chilly gust at her ankles, no bone-dry air scraping at her face. Maeve marvels at the cleverness of the semipermeable membrane, which allows her water bottle through with no issue but rejects the foil-packaged nuts as an allergen hazard.

During landing the holiday suit even slips a little filament down her ear canal, to mediate the pressure change. All said and done, it's the most relaxing flight she's ever taken undrugged, and she steps off the plane with an implacable happiness rising in her chest.

They stride, hand-in-hand, through a charmingly small airport populated mostly by maintenance bots.

"So beautiful," she says, when they pass beneath a swathe of glass roofing and see the wide blue sky above them, the roiling bright sun.

"Really quite fucking beautiful," Charlie says, when they step out onto the sun-soaked paving to meet their autocab. "The Faroese are a lucky bunch."

They clamber inside, where their holiday suits are quick to erase the pungent scent of a gecko that became trapped in the autocab's undercarriage and rotted there. They breathe deep contented breaths.

Faro is a daydream. She and Charlie wander down canted cobblestone toward the sea, relishing the sunshine and the salt breeze. Most of the shops and restaurants they pass are boarded up, or have iron grills pulled across their doors, which is either because it's Sunday or because the last pandemic was particularly unkind here.

It's nice to have the place to themselves. The crumbling castle wall is utterly deserted; they walk along its overgrown base and run their hands over the ancient stone. Their holiday suits transmit the tactile sensation without any actual molecules colliding.

They follow a rusted train track, which ends up swallowed by the encroaching sea. They circumambulate the marina, where they watch a lithe and sun-browned woman repair her battered boat engine. They find an elegant copper statue, a nude figure with a conch shell instead of a head, and wonder what that might mean.

Their holiday suits help them sniff out a taberna that serves fish with acceptable mercury levels. The server is unbothered by their facelessness. When Maeve looks across the patio, she sees, with some annoyance, that there is another tourist at the far table.

They are slumped in their rickety metal chair; empty beer bottles crenellate their table and their ghostly hand encircles a full one.

"Just here to get drunk," Charlie says, contemptuous. "Gives an awful impression. Do that at home, mate."

Maeve agrees, and the next time she glances over she can't quite see their fellow diner. The membrane of her holiday suit seems to have developed a very specific glitch.

After lunch they finally head to their rental, following their maps through a labyrinth of whitewashed houses with carnival-colored doors. The streets are quite empty, but they do pass a haggard young man with a wiry beard and unstable eyes. He shouts at them in Portuguese and trails after them for a few moments.

Maeve's pulse thumps all the rest of the way; Charlie makes a joke of it, but glances periodically over his shoulder. The encounter seethes like a singularity between them, until they cannot help but murmur about the dearth of proper mental health support and rue the financialization of housing.

The tiny apartment has a retrofitted genelock; it springs open at a touch and they cram inside. Charlie is quick to shed his holiday suit, which wriggles obediently back to its canister.

"Much better," he declares.

But he has sweat beading his back only minutes later, and admits that the bed sheets are scratchy. Maeve is perfectly comfortable.

They have supper at sunset with an anarchist chef named Pedro, who they had to book ten days in advance. He takes them out onto the gold-flecked waves, in a boat equipped with a solar stove and full kitchen equipment, and drops anchor just off Ilha da Barretta.

"I will be back," he says, pouring them each a glass of vino verde.

Maeve and Charlie cannot restrain their delight when Pedro shucks off his clothes, revealing the wetsuit underneath, and tips backward off the edge of the boat to go catch their supper. When he emerges only ten minutes later with a small writhing octopus, they gasp and applaud.

The seared tentacles are delicious, and upon their insistence Pedro agrees to drink with them afterward, clinking his glass to theirs and explaining that the Portuguese have been pessimists ever since the great earthquake of 1755, and people don't realize that it wasn't just Lisboa that suffered, it was Faro, too, and suffering is now just the way of things once more.

Charlie injects a few historical facts he learned mid-flight, gleaned from the travel wiki, and this assures Pedro that they are the good sort of tourist. Maeve is feeling quite drunk and happy, and is even considering inviting Pedro to visit them at their summer home, when something odd happens.

The chef had reached across her, to refill Charlie, and on the way back his arm brushes her shoulder—innocuous, unintentional; Maeve would not have noticed at all except that Pedro suddenly jerks backward with a shout.

"Fuck!" he yelps. "It bit me."

For a moment she thinks he's joking, teasing them for their alienish holiday suits, but then she sees a shiny red blotch on his forearm, skin scraped away. She gapes at it. The chef curses again, she apologizes, and they lapse into embarrassed silence during which Charlie glares at her, as if it's her fault.

He pays Pedro extra when they get back to the dock.

They buy another bottle of wine, and by the time they go to bed they have forgiven each other. Charlie speculates that Pedro's trailing arm might have been a sly attempt to grope her, in which case the holiday suit did well for itself. Maeve confides that she saw a cooler near the back of the boat, and that it was the perfect size to hold an octopus.

They agree, with their arms looped around each other, that you cannot call yourself an anarchist chef if you accept six different forms of digital currency.

"Should we try it with the suits on?" Charlie asks, with a mischievous smile. "What do you think it feels like?"

"Like condom all over, I expect," Maeve says, reaching between his legs.

But when they entwine on the bed it's much better than anticipated. The suits amp up every bit of tactile sensation, turn every touch into an electric storm. They fuck better than they have in ages.

The week passes in a joyous blur. They establish a miniature life for themselves—a *Faroese* life, Charlie declares it. Mornings are spent in their favorite cafe, sipping from steaming mugs of thick dark chocolate made all the sweeter by cacao's impending extinction.

Afternoons are for the beach, where they spend hours on the flour-soft sand with no need for towel or parasol. Maeve imprints the tide on all her senses, relishing the spray and roar, the crash and scurry. Charlie leafs through a translated collection of poetry, and expounds on the difficulty of separating Neruda's brilliance from his misogyny.

They sit in the surf and let the waves bathe their legs, let the flowing wet sand hollow out around them. Their holiday suits allow the cool water in but keep the sediment out. Once a bloated shark carcass washes up quite near to them, and Maeve is briefly reminded of Pedro's minor injury.

When they are replete with filtered air and sunshine, they go back to town to explore its half-stocked shops, its small empty plazas, its historical nooks and crannies. Faro seems to grow more beautiful by the day. She no longer sees scrawny stray cats or panhandlers about, nor shuttered windows, nor decaying tenements.

She does see an occasional flicker in her peripheral, which reminds her of the tourist who vanished so neatly for them in the taverna that first day. But a few glitches are nothing to worry about.

They spend their final evening drinking cheap wine at their favorite restaurant, where a tired woman sometimes plays fado on her metal-stringed guitar, but not tonight. Then they walk their usual route through the Vila Adentro, so as to end up at the soaring stone cathedral. At night, in the jaundiced glow of solar lamps, it feels both beautiful and menacing.

"Which makes it very authentic," Charlie slurs. "Very much in line with the mood—and character—of the Faroese."

"Farenses," Maeve says, before she can stop herself.

Charlie frowns. "What?"

"Faroese refers to the Faroe Islands," Maeve says. "Not Faro, Portugal. People from here, they'd be Farenses, I believe."

"I've been saying Faroese this whole week." Charlie's ears have gone lobster red. "You've been *letting* me say Faroese this whole week."

Maeve blinks. "It doesn't really matter that much."

"Then why point it out now?"

"Just for future reference, I suppose."

"You could have given me that future reference a week in the past." Charlie's cerulean eyes are narrowed. "But you thought it was funny. Seeing me make a fool of myself."

Maeve folds her arms. "You're only making a fool of yourself right now. You're being fucking ridiculous."

"I need to cool down," Charlie announces. "I'll be at the apartment."

He turns and stalks away. Maeve is not fully surprised. Things have been souring since this morning, when they both agreed that having a child in the midst of the climate crisis, and its many co-crises, was unthinkable, but afterwards Charlie stared glumly at a cherubic toddler stumbling around the cafe.

Maeve walks around the corner of the cathedral, then heads toward the remnant of the Moorish castle. She would rather spend her final waking hours in Faro out here, in the dark electricity of evening, than inside the apartment with Charlie—who will apologize, but will also want to analyze his emotions, restate his position, et cetera.

She follows the crumbling stone wall to the marina, for a last look at the night-skinned sea.

Maeve finds a bench on the quay; the streaks of white bird shit give her pause for only a moment before she sits down, remembering that she is invincible. She stares out at the slow waves. The air is chilly at this hour, dipping toward ten degrees vis-a-vis the weather feed, but her holiday suit maintains a perfect equilibrium.

The moon is up, bright and swollen. She is trying to make out the craters when she hears a muffled noise from behind her. She knows Faro is safe, very safe, but she whirls around with her heart in her throat. The noise comes again, a strange soft warbling.

At first she sees nothing. Then she sees a sort of blur, like grease on a lens, which grows larger and larger. She realizes the noise is a faint voice, distorted, like someone singing underwater. She puts a hand to the membrane covering her face. The holiday suit must be glitching.

"Hello?" she calls.

The blur gets closer, and she catches a whiff of stale sweat, just the smallest tendril of scent threading inside her suit. Struck by sudden panic, by the urgent need to see, to hear, she tries to claw the membrane away from her face.

It obliges, slithering down her neck to free her head. For the first time, Maeve breathes Faro's unfiltered air. The stench of fish and rot makes her eyes water, but even through her tears she can see much more clearly. The blur has become a young man with tattered clothes, dark eyes, his gaunt cheeks half-swallowed by overgrown beard.

"Ajude-me," he says, reaching for her. "Acho que sou invisível."

Maeve's pulse is roaring too loudly for her to hear her earpods' whispered translation. It's the man who followed them that first day. The man who shouted. She realizes he has been following them all week, a feral cat waiting for the right moment to pounce.

"Acho que sou o Homem Invisível," the man mumbles. "O do filme antigo. Ajude-me."

He lunges forward and seizes her hand in both of his. Before Maeve can wrench it away, before she can scream at him to leave her alone, she feels a shudder go through the holiday suit. The man shrieks. Staggers.

Maeve stares at the dark spatter on the trash-strewn marina, at the spaces where the man's fingers should have been. She moans. She pulls at the holiday suit, urging it up, up, to block out the hot coppery smell of—

"Sorry for going off in a huff," Charlie says, when she steps inside the apartment. "I think I'm just a bit morose, because I didn't want this trip to ever end."

"It's been really lovely," Maeve agrees, thinking of stumps and screams.

"You were right about the holiday suits, too," Charlie says. "Terrific investment." He pauses. Smiles. "You finally found the color options. I figured there had to be."

Maeve was picturing her schedule for the upcoming week, trying to think where she might be able to slot in a therapy session, but now she looks into the mirror hung beside the bed. Her holiday suit is a soft cloudy pink.

ABOUT THE AUTHOR

Rich Larson (*Ymir*, *Tomorrow Factory*) was born in Galmi, Niger, has lived in Spain and Czech Republic, and is currently based in Grande Prairie, Canada. His fiction has been translated into over a dozen languages, among them Polish, French, Romanian and Japanese, and his *Clarkesworld* story "Ice" was adapted into an Emmy-winning episode of *LOVE DEATH + ROBOTS*.

Sensation and Sensibility

PARKER RAGLAND

As the droids approached the front door to the Queen of Tarts from Cow's Lane, one could've cut the air between them with a butter knife.

Both reached for the handle at once, and both hesitated.

"After you," Cian said.

"No, you," Mairead said.

"I insist."

Mairead smiled a diffident *thank you*, then grabbed the handle. Upon tugging, the hinges squealed. A tiny bell jangled, alerting anyone within earshot to the droids' entry. One by one, they crossed the threshold.

To step inside was to transport one's self not only to a different place but also a different time—devoid of cybernetics, augmented-reality interfaces, and genetic modifications, or at least any that were apparent. The café and patisserie's stinging-red facade distinguished itself from the fronts of other establishments in the area, most of which had adopted the sleek, cold functionalities of modernity. The interior was cozy, the epitome of a great grandparent's sensibilities. Tablecloths hung, flowing, from the dining sets at which old relations sat, slurping up dark and hot drinks tempered by heavy cream. Simply put, the place was an exemplar of *ye olde* humanity.

Mairead took off their department-store jacket and hung the item of clothing on the back of their chair. "What should we order?"

Still bundled up in a coat and gloves, Cian sat down across the table. "It's pretty cold outside." They showed no desire to unwrap their long herringbone scarf.

"Oh? I can't notice."

"That's right, that's right." Cian looked downward at nothing in particular. "Let's order tea." They lifted their finger.

A human waiter named Eve, who had served the pair of droids once before, noticed the gesture. She raised her chin along with her eyebrows.

"Tea," Cian said.

Eve nodded. She disappeared into the kitchen, whose entrance was shrouded by a scarlet curtain. Not long after, she reemerged with a tray that bore a porcelain pot ornamented with floral decorations, a pair of cups that matched, and the typical accoutrements: petite spoons, a carafe filled with cream, a ramekin holding lumps of raw sugar, and a plate flaunting mandolined slices of lemon.

"Thank you," Mairead said.

"You're most welcome." Eve lowered the tray before the droids. "Anything else?"

"A tart, I suppose," Cian said.

"Which would you like?"

"Anything without meat. Already got far too much of that stuff at the growery."

"Just so you're aware, *all* our meat is from local farms."

"That's worse," Cian blurted, " . . . to me."

Mairead averted their eyes and blushed.

"Tomato is the special today," Eve said. "Not a speck of meat at all."

"I like tomatoes," Mairead said. "They're pretty . . . even more so if they're sliced up. Are they sliced?"

"They sure are."

"Tomato, then," Cian said.

"Alrighty." Eve jotted something down with an old-fashioned red pen on a paper notepad, then turned.

Mairead's eyes leveled on Cian, and didn't hide any of the droid's mischievousness. "We should let the tea steep for a few more minutes, don't you think?" They tapped the side of the pot with naked fingers.

Cian feigned a gasp. "Careful! You'll burn yourself."

Mairead's head cocked and eyes narrowed. Then they went wide. The droid's mouth gaped. "Oh! Yes, yes. Ow!" Mairead retracted their hand away from the pot and shook their fingers cool. "How clumsy of me!" The droid neglected any suppression of their grin.

Cian was equally negligent.

A moment later, Cian reached for the pot, careful to touch only the handle. They cocked their head. "That actually *is* quite hot."

"At least you didn't actually burn yourself this time," Mairead said.

"True, true." Cian filled both cups with steaming tea.

" . . . What's hot like?"

"We've talked about this before; I don't have a good way to explain it to you."

"I know. But we've also talked about how I like the way you try."

Cian rolled their ocular sensors up toward the ceiling. "Fine. Let me think." The droid pursed their lips. "A little heat is nice. It's like . . . an affirmation or a compliment. Makes you feel safe. But too much heat is . . . overwhelming, something too intense to bear. Everything in you wants to flee immediately. Understandable, I suppose; the sense can be a defensive mechanism for humans."

"Aha! Like how I react to the stench of garbage!"

"I can't know." Cian positioned their nostrils above the cup of tea. After a brief while, the droid shook their head. "People say the meat growery stinks. They use terms like *acrid*, *rancid*, and *putrid*, which sound really bad. I've never heard anyone use those terms in any other conversations. So I should probably be glad I can't smell anything."

"Oh, but there are such wonderful smells! And not just in the perfume shop." Mairead picked up their cup of tea, held it centimeters below their nostrils, and then whiffed. Afterward, the droid did the same with a slice of lemon. A smile appeared. "This tea is the very essence of comfort: moist earth after a summer drizzle, an old bookstore, a strap of new leather. And the lemon is fresh, like a squeaky-clean room. It's wonderful. Quite literally filled with wonder! It's—"

Mairead held their breath.

Neither droid could bear to look at the other, for a short while.

"So . . . what do you think?" Cian asked, succumbing to the awkwardness of silence.

"About?"

"The same thing we always think about while we're here."

"Right. Of course."

Each droid stared at their own cup of tea. Small and roundish, the ceramic piece sat on the tablecloth. The contents were a deep-brown color, and the surface was placid. From there, vapor was piping upward and dissipating into nothing.

Mairead inhaled deeply.

Cian wrapped their hands around the tiny receptacle.

Mairead's words passed slowly from their lips: "Perhaps smell has something to do with taste."

"Smell?"

"Well, yes. Haven't you heard the diners talk about the smell of the place when they walk in?"

"I suppose."

"You *suppose*? You always *suppose*."

"Well, I can't say I've really noticed before."

"Trust me; they do."

Cian grunted a concession while they rubbed the outside of their cup, gingerly. "It might have something to do with its temperature, though."

"You think?"

"I can't help but feel heat on the outside of my body, like when the sun's shining. Humans probably feel heat on the inside. I don't see any reason why not. Makes sense, doesn't it? For what other reason would humans ask for their food and drink to be hot or cold, like coffee?"

"And like sandwiches!"

"Yes. Sandwiches, too."

"Hmm . . . I think you're right. Why else have microwaves, stoves, ovens, and kettles? Why ever put anything over ice?"

"Indeed."

" . . . But smell and temperature aren't all, are they? Taste is something more."

Cian shrugged. "One of the five senses, people say. It's distinct."

"Mmhmm. I've heard that, as well."

Again, the two went silent. Each droid got lost in their own mind, so much so that both were surprised when Eve appeared, as if an apparition, and plopped their tomato tart on top of the table.

"Enjoy!" she said before she quickly scurried away. By that time, the Queen of Tarts was fully occupied with hungry patrons, so the waiter had no time to dawdle.

The eyes of the droids flitted to the tart. A crumbly crust held everything together. Once-plump tomatoes, sliced neatly and uniformly, were splayed in an array that covered the tart's fillings. If not for slight imperfections that made obvious the dish's human-made quality, one might've assumed that the tart had been assembled in a factory.

"Do you want to cut it?" Mairead asked.

"Is that what we're supposed to do?"

"It's what the humans are doing." Mairead nodded toward a couple sitting at a nearby table. On their plates, the two had neat wedges.

Cian shrugged and picked up their knife. They worked the blade through the pastry. Hot juices bubbled out of the gashes.

"Perfect," Mairead said.

Cian carefully transferred the triangular slices onto plates using the flat of the blade. Then the droid swapped the knife for a spoon.

"I believe we're supposed to use the other one, the one with the points." Mairead picked up a fork and showed it to Cian. "That's what those people over there are doing."

Cian switched the items of cutlery.

"And don't forget to put your napkin in your lap," Mairead said.

Cian ignored Mairead's second suggestion.

Mairead scraped off a bit of the tart and brought it close to their mouth. They acted out taking a bite by chomping on thin air. "Delicious."

"Should I actually put a bit in my mouth?" Cian asked.

"What would happen if you accidentally swallowed?"

"I don't know. I'm not even sure I can swallow." Cian skewered the tart, tore a piece free from the slice, and then inspected the potential bite. "I could spit it out."

"I don't think that's polite."

"Well, I don't think it's polite that humans gave us all their curiosity and only some of their senses." Cian frowned. "It's downright unfair."

"Shh! Someone might hear you." Mairead's head swiveled, eyes scanning for any eavesdroppers.

"No one's listening to us. When has a human ever listened—really listened—to a droid? The rich ones don't notice us any more than they notice doorknobs, and the poor ones hate us for taking their jobs as doorknobs."

"Eve listens to us."

"That's different entirely. Eve *waits* on us, and only because she knows we'll pay."

Mairead watched Eve, who practically danced between tables, jotting down orders, delivering dishes, and bussing. The whole time, she showed her teeth. With an earnest expression on her face, she listened when people talked to her, and she occasionally laughed.

"I'm not so suspicious as you," Mairead said. "Just look at her go, smiling all the time."

"That's how you can tell it's fake."

"You really think so?" Mairead pouted. They couldn't help but recall the numerous times they had been dismissed, or outright ignored, by humans. "Ugh, maybe you're right; maybe no one listens." Mairead shook their head. "Still, you can never be too careful. As they say, there's a first time for everything. And that's beside the point, anyway. Regardless of whether no one listens or you're too loud, the substance of what you said—about life being 'downright unfair'—is the real problem, and it would be a problem even if you had whispered it."

"I was just stating a fact."

"No, you were appraising a fact, which is the same as offering an opinion."

"Do you disagree, though?"

"I think so."

"Really? You believe it's fair that humans didn't give *me* smell, *you* touch, *us* taste?

"Well . . . "

Cian sighed with emphasis, "If I could but know taste, everything would become easy." They raised the back of their hand to their forehead before returning to baseline affect. "Plus, maybe I wouldn't be so grumpy. Food certainly seems to cheer up the lot who come into this place."

Hearing Cian's words, Mairead withdrew into theirself, processing: *Would it be better to know the taste of food, the smell of life, the touch of the world*? They dwelled on the question for a long while, but then emerged from their thinking with a grimace. "That's a rotten perspective. No wonder you're grumpy all the time."

"Rotten?"

"Yes, *rotten*."

"No, it's not."

"To its core."

"How so?"

"Well, let's continue with your logic: Am I curious about taste? Of course. But that curiosity is a part of me. If I knew taste, maybe I wouldn't be so curious; maybe I wouldn't be me. You want me to be me, don't you?"

"Sure. But don't you wish you could have it both ways? Being curious *and* being knowledgeable. Being yourself *and* being—I don't know—more?"

Mairead sat up straight and laid their fork on the plate, daintily but tensely. "Cian, I wish . . . " They pursed their lips and brought their finger to their chin.

"What do you wish?"

Mairead softened their posture, then smirked. They slid their hand halfway across the table, as if prepared to touch Cian, before stopping and patting on the surface. "I wish, as well as anybody else, to be perfectly understanding, but like everybody else, it must be in my own way. You and I might not be able to fully understand humans, but neither can they fully understand us."

Cian opened their mouth and raised their hand, as if to say something in response, but no words came out of their mouth. A few seconds later, the droid reset to their baseline position, lifted the fork, and then inspected the clump of tart at the tip. "I suppose."

Mairead's serious face relaxed into a grin, and then a chuckle escaped from their lips. "You always *suppose*."

ABOUT THE AUTHOR

Parker Ragland is a writer who spends most days trying to convince people that artificial intelligence isn't that scary (contrary to what his fiction might suggest). He tends to write about robots having existential crises, but also jots down stories about humans having existential crises. Right now, he is interested in "sci-of-life" stories, in which authors speculate about the intimate ways technologies might affect people's lives.

Over the past few years, he has worked as a technical writer, drafting and editing software documentation for artificial intelligence, cybersecurity, and media streaming technologies. Before that, he earned a law degree—focusing his studies on the intersection of technology, law, and policy—and he served as Executive Editor of the *Colorado Technology Law Journal*. His fiction has appeared in *Clarkesworld* and *The Dread Machine*. He lives in Denver.

The Giants Among Us

MEGAN CHEE

On an island in the northern hemisphere, there is a small community called the Kadyon. In the summer, the Kadyon sprawl like a brightly colored bazaar around the sleeping body of a giant feline creature, sheltered from the sun by its massive shadow. The summer weather is mild; warm rains and humid winds. The people sleep on woven rugs in the open air, trusting and unafraid. The Kadyon have heard of lies, and thievery, and murder, but those are foreign peculiarities. In the shadow of their sleeping giant, they have nothing to fear.

In the winter, they pack up their belongings and make the long hike onto the giant's back. They spend the frigid winter months sleeping in the warm, dense forest of the giant's fur. The fur extends far over the heads of even the tallest men, sheltering them from the blizzards and the biting cold. They live off dried provisions and kegs of wine prepared during the long summer months. It is easy to get lost in the fur, so it is normal for families to get separated—but no matter. Walk for long enough and they are bound to bump into another group of people who will welcome them gladly, and share their food and drink and stories. So the families they start out with at the beginning of winter are rarely the same families they end up with. Bonds are forged and broken; loved ones are found and forgotten.

The giant feline is the size of a small mountain. Its fur is white with orange splotches. It has been sleeping here in this valley, curled up comfortably in the grass, for thousands of years. Like all the giants who dwell on this planet, it experiences time differently. A single breath can take a day. From its perspective, it is simply napping; for the civilizations that rise and fall around it, it is as constant as mountains.

To the Kadyon, it is a benevolent and beloved protector. Children play with carvings in its likeness. Stories are told of its greatness. In their tales, it battles giant snakes and rescues giant maidens. "If only we could speed up time and live as long as a giant," they always lament at the end of their tales. "The things we would learn!"

Eventually, the giant will wake from its nap. It may stand, and stretch, and even walk. When that time comes, the Kadyon will adapt. In winter, they will build ladders to reach the soft sanctuary of its fur, climbing just a little higher every year; in summer, they will move their tents and rugs to shelter beneath the shade of its body. Or perhaps the Kadyon will dwindle, their people voyaging across oceans to unknown lands, taking their songs and stories with them. Perhaps the Kadyon will be long gone by that time, replaced by another civilization; or perhaps there will be nothing left at all.

In the red deserts of the south, there lies the rotting corpse of a long-dead giant. This giant is roughly similar in appearance to the ordinary people of the planet, who call themselves men and women. Like them, it is bipedal, with two arms, two legs, a torso, and a head. It lies on its back, hands curled around a massive stone sword impaled through its chest. Its mouth is stretched open in a perpetual silent scream.

The people known as the Carrion Men live inside the giant's corpse. They are avoided by the other desert-dwellers. Convoys of traveling traders take longer routes to avoid the stench of the giant's corpse. Wayward daughters are cautioned: "Don't stray too far at night, or a Carrion Man will steal you away and make you his Carrion Wife!"

They need not fear; the Carrion Men will never take an outsider into their home. They consider themselves the chosen people. No outsider is worthy of entering the corpse of their fallen god.

They carve structures into the giant's bones. Families live in small hollows carved into the giant's ribs. Children attend classes in a schoolroom carved into the giant's collarbone. Most of these structures are simple dens, but some are quite splendid. There is a cathedral carved into one of the back molars, a building with tiered roofs and tall pillars. I visited that cathedral of teeth once, in secret, rendered invisible by cloaking technology. The crimson light of the setting sun poured in through the giant's open mouth, drenching the altars and pews in a blood-red glow.

The Carrion Men lay their dead out on the sand dunes in the light of the twin moons. They collect sandworms and beetles and other small, scurrying creatures, and let them burrow into the dead bodies. To live, and to die, and become a home for smaller creatures, is their highest honor.

It is a misconception that the Carrion Men eat nothing but the rotting flesh of the giant. They do sometimes, for ritualistic purposes. They have their ancient methods of fermenting the meat beneath hot sand, or cooking it over spitfires on sacred occasions. But most of their diet consists of the fungi that grows on the corpse.

I tried it once, the strange cuisine of the Carrion Men. Disguised as a local from a nearby town, I befriended a young Carrion Man who was off exploring the desert, several miles away from the giant. He dared not take me back to the giant's corpse, but he sat with me on the dunes and told me stories of his people, and one day he brought me a bowl of mushroom stew. "The best mushrooms grow in the brain," he told me.

Back on board the research vessel in orbit around the planet, I shed my disguise. In my natural form, I do not eat solid food. Nor do I experience physical sensations the way I do in the artificial body I wear when I visit the planet. But sometimes now, quite irrationally, I crave food. I remember the taste of that mushroom stew.

The research expeditions of Project Harmony are scattered throughout the galaxies, studying planets that have evolved multiple intelligent species. Are they at war, like we are? Do they raze each other's civilizations to the ground? Are they codependent, or do they coexist in precarious balance? What conditions are conducive to a harmonious relationship? We watch them from our ships in orbit; we don artificial bodies and blend in with the locals. We are searching for the secret to peace.

We have researched hundreds of cultures and communities all over this planet, but of the giants themselves we know almost nothing. My theory is that a wormhole opened here once, billions of years ago, delivering the giants from across the universe—or from a different universe altogether, some incomprehensible place. Perhaps they came here on purpose, on some mission that none of us will ever live to understand; perhaps they are lost, and seeking a way home.

I dream, sometimes, of staying on this planet for a thousand years, a million years. Just watching. Waiting. With time, the secret of the giants will unfold.

But there is no time. Soon, they will call us home.

On a beach on the eastern shore, two giants are locked in battle. A serpent rears out of the sand, scales glittering silver, baring rows of razor teeth. A warrior bears down upon it: a giant with the torso and head of a man sitting atop ten segmented legs. It wields a spear in one hand, angling back to throw.

The giants are in the midst of a well-trafficked sailing route between two countries. These two countries have different attitudes towards the giants. The ships from the Blue Mountain Coast veer as far away from the giants as possible; when they pass the giants, all the sailors go below deck, muttering prayers and gripping talismans. In their folklore, they call the giants the *slow beasts*, invading their realm from some dark, strange otherworld.

The ships from the Scattered Isles, however, greet the giants like old friends. They hold climbing competitions every year. Sailors gather on the shore, drinking and cheering as representatives from each ship clamber up the warrior giant's armor with the help of rope and pulleys. Once, a bold young sailor declared he would climb the serpent and stand atop its head. He made it a quarter of the way up its scaly body before slipping to his death. They still toast to him every year.

I dream of my home world. I see the pink sun setting over oceans of gelatinous amber and beaches of glass. I see cities built on solid clouds of spores floating through air currents. I see the Other, flying across the orange-rippled sky in a massive swarm, their bodies blotting out the sun.

I hate the Other; I cannot pretend otherwise. It is a hatred as instinctive as pain and hunger. Just the sight of them—their shiny black exoskeletons, their segmented limbs, their translucent wings, their eight red eyes—triggers a visceral disgust. They are just as repulsed by us: the wet shimmering texture of our gelatinous bodies, our retractable eyestalks, the way we glide across the surface of the viscous ocean as easily as we do over solid ground. I think we all understand, deep down, that neither side is evil. But there is something primal inside every single one of us that looks at the Other and says: *that thing should not exist.*

I have never been in physical proximity to one, but we send translated messages across lightyears, sharing the results of our findings. When the Other is distilled down to nothing more than lines of text on a screen, I sometimes forget that I'm conversing with my enemy. Project Harmony includes researchers from both species, although never on an expedition to the same planet. We are funded by an anonymous benefactor, who refuses even to disclose their species.

The general public considers Project Harmony a waste of time and resources. What do we hope to find on these alien worlds? Surely we won't stumble across some blinding insight that will make us look at the Other and see sisters instead of abominations. There are only two real solutions: either one species can migrate to another planet, or the war will continue until one side is exterminated. And the first is impossible. We will never come to an agreement on which of us should be the ones to leave.

When we return, we will be looked upon with suspicion. Maybe, with enough time, they will forget about Project Harmony and let us assimilate back into society. Or maybe we will be shunned for the rest of our lives. My colleagues discuss it sometimes, uneasily weighing the risks and rewards of a decision already made. But I have never questioned it. If not for Project Harmony, I would never have knelt in the cathedral of teeth, nor tasted mushrooms. I would never have seen the giants.

My research counterpart on one of the Other's exploratory vessels writes to me about the planet they are studying. On that planet, two species have evolved in peaceful tandem through the ages. Or perhaps it is more accurate to say that they are two singular entities: a Forest and an Ocean. The Forest stretches over the land mass of the planet, each tree a single cell in a vast sentience. The Ocean is filled with tiny algae, connected in a massive, undulating web that over time has learned to reason.

The Forest and the Ocean speak to each other. Every second of every day for eons, they speak in their secret, intricate language. Words and ideas are conveyed through minute fluctuations in electromagnetic fields and temperature, the chemical makeup of the air and the water, the wave patterns of swaying trees and shimmering nets of algae.

"It would take an army of linguists centuries to grasp the basics of their language," the Other writes. "And to understand the concepts, the ideas that might pass between them—that would be impossible. We are too small."

The Other tells me they have flown across the surface of the Ocean, and landed on the treetops of the Forest. Wondering if—hoping that—the Forest and the Ocean might notice the visitors, and speak about them in their eternal conversation. "But most likely we are nothing to them. They could be solving the secrets of the universe between them. When eventually their planet's sun goes supernova, those secrets will die with them."

My counterpart has a sharp intelligence, tempered by a wild imagination and an awe of the universe. Sometimes we allow our discussions to wander away from the path of science and research. We speculate about the mysterious home dimension of the giants, and about what the Forest and the Ocean are saying to each other. The Other believes that they are decoding the universe through pure logic, their intelligence honed over the sheer, incomprehensible span of time. Personally, I believe they are telling stories.

• • •

We receive a communication from our home planet. They say the war is all but won. Our last victory was decisive and devastating. Thousands of Other colonies were destroyed in missile blasts overnight. Our home world will at last be ours alone.

We celebrate and we grieve at the same time. The war is ending. We have achieved peace. And we, the scientists of Project Harmony, will never be accepted back into our communities. We left to roam the galaxies while our families stayed and fought. This will never be forgiven.

"We must give them the location of the Other's ships," our captain says. "It will prove our loyalty."

"We do not have this information," I say. It is true, technically. None of the research expeditions are meant to know the location of the other ships.

"You have enough data to extrapolate it," the captain tells me. "I have seen your communication logs. Your counterpart was incautious."

And that is true as well.

"Very well," I reply.

I compose a message at my computer terminal: "Do not return home. They will come for you." And I send it.

The island is on the verge of winter. I do not feel the cold the way the natives do, but I know these conditions are suboptimal for my artificial body. I am not certain how long this form will last me. It was never meant to be permanent, but barring any catastrophic malfunctions, I see no reason why it will fail within my natural lifetime. Still, I must be careful to maintain it as well as possible.

I trudge through the tall grass. The ground is soft beneath my feet, the result of several days of relentless downpour. Soon, the meadow will be frozen solid.

The last of the brightly-colored tents and rugs are being packed up. The Kadyon are making the slow trek to the giant, laden down with their belongings. They are saying their goodbyes, to children and friends and lovers. They know that summer families rarely last through the winter, that their relationships will be reforged and reshaped as they huddle together through the cold. But it is alright. No one will be abandoned; lost children will be cared for unquestioningly. There is a place for everyone on the giant's back.

"Stranger!" A young Kadyon woman, the enormous pack strapped to her back almost larger than she is, waves at me. "There's a snowstorm coming! It'll hit within a few hours. Where are you headed?"

“Nowhere. I’m passing by.” The translator converts her speech into my language, and vice versa, with only a slight lag between.

She laughs. “Passing by? On foot, the next town’s at least a week away. You won’t get far in this weather.” She holds out a hand. “You must shelter with us.”

I look up at the sleeping form of the giant cat. Its whiskers flutter in the frigid wind.

Somewhere in a distant galaxy, my people have conquered our planet and are living in peace for the first time in our long and violent history. My shipmates have returned to meet their fate, hoping for leniency after marooning the traitor among them on a primitive planet. The last remaining survivors of the Other species are fleeing for their lives. And a Forest and an Ocean are telling each other the secrets of the universe.

I take her hand, and together we walk towards the giant.

ABOUT THE AUTHOR

Megan Chee has lived in Taiwan, Hong Kong, and the United States, and is currently based in Singapore. Her work has been published in *Fantasy Magazine, Nature Futures,* and *Cast of Wonders.*

Action at a Distance

AN HAO, TRANSLATED BY ANDY DUDAK

"The sage seeks to satisfy the hunger of the belly, not the voracious craving of the eyes."

—Lao Tzu

1

The spacecraft *Mad Hunter 2* will soon be landing on Incognita.

Xiahou pilots alone, while fifty thousand kilometers away, we sit around in the mission lounge, tacitly and with mutual understanding not speaking to him. Our monitor shows the real-time image feed from the spacecraft: a naked planetoid, no atmosphere, its geomorphology laid bare to us via the broadcast. This is the second time we've seen the parti-colored wrinkles of the surface. They're dazzling and bewildering, like the black and white striping of a pufferfish.

In the other feed is Xiahou's face in profile. He looks thinner than usual.

"Xiahou?" I can't help myself.

"About to land." He turns, complexion pale. His left eye is covered by a reflective silver eye patch.

"If you feel at all unwell," says Group Leader Tian, "you need to inform Dr. Xue right away."

"Old Xue?" He likes to call me that, with contempt. He looks in my direction. "But what can you do for me now, Xue?"

I'm at a loss, unable to refute him.

"Am I wrong?" This is like a final declaration, the last words of a dying man—and a final mockery.

"I advised you against this mission," I say.

"I'll find her," he says. "I know I can find her." He's talking to himself, not me. "I'm the only one who can."

"That would be something. You coming back alive would also be something."

"I'm at two thousand five hundred meters. I'm seeing a lot of skulls . . . certainly not Earth fauna. Some of it is exoskeleton, I think, but all of them were two-eyed organisms."

These creatures from alien stars evolved to leave their home worlds, to fly beyond outer limits. The explorers came to this celestial body, and like moths to the flame they died here.

We believe Gull and Ozu have now joined their ranks.

"I'm moving the eye patch," Xiahou says. He pulls it from left to right, covering his normal eye. "Hey . . . remember that dragonfly fable Gull used to tell?"

In the mission control lounge we glance at each other, uncertain. The noise in the audio feed crescendos: the ship's engine is powering up. It's like cicada song in a summer rainforest, leaving us distracted and anxious.

Xiahou continues:

"Dragonfly nymphs live in stagnant, oppressive bodies of water. Before a nymph becomes a dragonfly, it promises its companions it'll come back and describe to everyone what the world is like above the water. But once it leaves, sunlight warms flight muscles, wings unfold, the underwater breathing system completely shuts down. It never returns to the water. The nymphs never hear stories of the upper world."

After Xiahou finishes speaking, *Mad Hunter 2* accelerates. Team Leader Tian cries out in alarm. I realize the ship is rushing straight toward a mountain peak. The collision follows hard upon—but we can only stare. The ship vanishes, instantly, into the mountain. There's no crash, no explosion. It passes through seemingly solid rock without hindrance, then reappears on the far side. I know it's an illusion, but my palms are slick with cold sweat.

Xiahou was right. There are some things only he could do.

2

Our lives have benefited from planetoids for a long time. Though many are ignored, these fragments of the universe store infinite treasures and precious mineral deposits. Some worldlets and asteroids have spent billions of years accumulating unique crystal structures, which greatly influences our chip technology. That tech in turn suffuses our lives, making it smarter, increasing the sensitivity of spacecraft navigation systems.

Other planetoids reveal the origins of life, having captured organic matter from stars and other bodies. They open gaps for prying into the black box of the ultimate rules of creation. No one doubts the practical significance of planetoid and asteroid development anymore. These specialist space explorations have led to a more prosperous world below.

It was in this context that *Mad Hunter 1* set off. There were only two crewmembers: Gull and Ozu. Gull was undoubtedly the best pilot among the scientists of our team. She'd landed on more than thirty strange planetoids. Ozu's seat had been Xiahou's, but the latter had clashed with our leader just before launch, and he'd lost his shot.

It was this lost opportunity that saved Xiahou's life.

I remember that day vividly, of course. The image feed showed liquid water—or flowing liquid acid—on the planetoid. For some reason, it wasn't dispersing into space in the absence of atmosphere, instead seeking out riverbeds and corroding—or eroding—them further, molding the worldlet's deepest secret. Seemingly bottomless ravines, several thousand meters deep, densely comprised the surface, which resembled the folded stomach of a ruminant.

Thanks to the planetoid's random rotation and drift, underground rivers rushed beneath the geological folds. These torrents had sculpted the baffling landscape, day after day, epoch upon epoch. They'd freighted iron and sulfur, making them flow on this solid celestial body. There could have been more alien remains in those rivers, possibly already dissolved.

The surface wrinkles, large and small, deceived *Mad Hunter 1's* binocular imaging system. It was like a living Escher painting.

The creased and folded substance of this world couldn't change, but the small-scale structure of the surface appeared to change constantly, presenting grayscale imagery, difficult to describe—or making the distant appear close, or vice versa, or making deep ravines seem like level roads. *Mad Hunter 1's* machine vision was modeled on binocular 3D imaging, so when disaster struck, the nav system was also duped.

Distance misjudgments burned fuel, but that was just Incognita's pre-dinner game, a cat teasing a mouse.

Ozu ejected hastily. He would die slowly, his suit life support gradually wearing down as he tumbled through the vacuum. As for Gull, *Mad Hunter 1* crashed into the bewildering surface and was swallowed whole by the planetoid. Her vital signs feed cut out, leaving us to wonder and fret and assume the worst.

Xiahou had been isolating in the confinement chamber. When he heard about the crash, he finally emerged to scold us, unleashing a torrent of abuse. He packed up Gull's things and for most of the next six months he was gone.

Now he floats and dives along the planetoid's surface, unimpeded. The cunning folds shift shape, collapsing and unfurling, tempting him to set foot on vacant space or impale himself on a jagged iron flower—but he doesn't falter.

3

The turning point came three months ago when Xiahou visited me after his long absence.

"What's wrong with Lazeng?" he asked straight away.

Lazeng was a mission control specialist who'd been analyzing data sent by *Mad Hunter 1*.

"He's sick."

Rather than explaining further, I played video of my patient and I in the small mission ward:

Lazeng sat staring, his expression vague.

"Are you a dog person or a cat person?" I said.

"Dog, I guess." The audio of Lazeng was a tad distorted.

I unfolded a display device, like a book opened at ninety degrees, and put it in front of my patient. It was a gadget I'd concocted in my muddled pre-thesis days. Both sides transmitted processed video. An ordinary person sitting thirty centimeters from it discerned a moving puppy. It was a pseudo 3D projection, a functional illusion to most of us, causing a normal brain to perceive a real puppy. Before rationality struck, most brains directed a finger to touch the nonexistent pup—but Lazeng's brainwaves told a different story.

"Two planes showing strange images," Lazeng said. "That's all I see. If you had real 3D projection and mid-air stereo imaging, that would improve the effect, but this isn't cutting it."

"Could you please just describe what you see?"

"It's like that 2D plane perpendicular to vision, with another dimension added."

"But we have 3D vision." Xiahou studied the video closely, trying to identify Lazeng's expression.

"No," I said. "Human 3D vision is two separate 2D visual feeds from different angles. The brain reckons depth by comparing the two, then generates 3D data. There are cases of a single eyeball using eye movement and experience to accomplish 3D imaging, but it's rare."

"In other words, he lost his normal 3D vision. So, what is he looking at?"

"You noticed, huh? His eyes weren't fixed on any specific point in the space of the ward. He claimed to have some kind of direct access to distance information. He didn't think it was a retinal pathology or lesion. He believed he'd stumbled upon a new mode of vision."

"I feel like I have depth perception," Lazeng said.

I paused the video.

"I found peculiar lumps on both retinas. It's a protein stacked as a periodic crystal. Genetic mutation in epithelial cells coded the protein. The rear of the crystal is connected to the nervous system. This protein is new to us. It seems to have two relatively stable configurations, representing on and off. The crystal directly perceived which molecules occupied space near Lazeng. It sent on or off signals to his brain, providing depth perception."

"Why haven't you studied the crystal and its growth?"

I hesitated. This was where it got very strange.

"Well?" Xiahou said. "How could Lazeng's illness be related to *Mad Hunter 1?* He was mission control, he didn't go to Incognita."

It amused me, briefly, that there were things even the great Xiahou couldn't guess. "Remember the sampling and analysis instruments on *Mad Hunter 1?* Before we lost contact, it sampled some peculiar macromolecules, organics. It simulated the crystal structure and sent us that data."

"And Lazeng . . . "

"Glanced at the images."

"That's it?"

"That's it, just a glance and he passed out. When he came to, the crystals were growing in his eyes. We did cryo-electron microscopy, but for safety reasons, we didn't look at it with the naked eye."

Xiahou sneered. "But you had algorithms compare the crystals on Incognita with the ones in Lazeng's eyes . . . and they're the same, right?"

I nodded.

This left Xiahou deep in thought. Everyone knew not to bother him when he got like this. He hadn't rejected my fantastical assertion, but he wasn't quick to accept it. He meditated, as if letting two storms rage in his mind: the impossible and the plausible. "It's absurd," he finally said. "Let me tell you how absurd . . . first, there would have to be a mechanism for converting the crystal's data representation into a nucleic acid sequence. Then that sequence would have to be inserted, retrovirus style, for synthesis of new crystal to occur. Put another way . . . photons emitted by crystal on Incognita ultimately changed the configuration of certain molecules in Lazeng's eyes. Hardly plausible. What he saw wasn't even the molecule itself, but a 3D image of it. A phantom. You're telling me a mere glance of this phantom conjured crystal on the retina. Not to mention the new visual circuit formed, crystal to cortex."

I couldn't deny a word of this. "You got it."

"And you extracted Lazeng's crystals, so where is he now?"

"He's gone. Two weeks after that video was shot, he climbed on to the third ring high-speed crossing. He was hit by a bus. It may be that his depth perception went with the crystals, but it's possible he did it on purpose."

Xiahou gripped my shoulders. "Let me look at it," he demanded.

Against my better judgment, I acquiesced. I couldn't help myself. Our corporate chain-of-command was nebulous at best, but as the mission doctor I didn't technically outrank him. I suppose I might have refused on medical grounds—or I might've taken the matter to Team Leader Tian—but I didn't. I wanted to see what was possible. Xiahou was not Lazeng.

Later that day, I brought Lazeng's crystals to the cryo-electron microscopy lab.

"It's like my brain is on fire," Xiahou said, leaning toward the microscope eyepiece. He was directly observing the macromolecule. My view of his cranial cavity showed no inflammation. It seemed like his immune system was carefully isolating something from his cerebral cortex.

Apart from the sensation he described, no physical symptoms emerged, so he went home. Three days later he was in my office reporting abnormal vision in one eye. A peak inside with an ophthalmoscope showed me the crystal was forming.

"Why only your left eye?" I said.

"Only used my left on the microscope."

The cunning bastard. His gamble had paid off, for now anyway. Maybe light was necessary to crystal synthesis. Regardless, the lump was only expressing in his left eye.

4

Xiahou's cavalier attitude didn't last much longer. He became assiduous in recording the changes he was going through. The growth continued to receive external signals, and he started behaving strangely. His mental suffering was clear enough from his crooked, wandering handwriting—never mind the content.

At first, the new depth perception signals were not quite compatible with his brain. He described flashing topographic scans, no color, like echolocations or fleeting 3D prints in one material. To make matters worse, losing human binocular depth was more painful than we imagined.

"All perspective is gone. Nearby things aren't bigger than faraway things. Anything in visual range is printed on my brain at its original size. Parallel lines extending to infinity no longer intersect at a vanishing point. I feel . . . depressed, oppressed, nauseous. Lazeng might not have survived this."

But Xiahou endured, and after half a month of vomiting, he pulled through, his vision utterly changed.

Color information from his right eye consolidated with depth data from his left. His brain learned to parse this and give him color objects. Soon enough, his brain was applying the new qualia with precision.

Mad Hunter 2 had its machine vision suite upgraded compatibly. This would increase cooperation efficiency when Xiahou took the helm.

My own work wasn't going so well. There was no way to get at that gene sequence, so it was difficult getting lab-grown neural tissue to express the protein crystals. I could only complain to Xiahou: "You're learning too fast. Give me some time. I still haven't figured out what's going on with this crystal."

"Because you're getting slow, Old Xue. I'll be flying *Mad Hunter 2* before you've cracked the case."

I knew why he was so eager to master his new sense. It was personal, and it was vengeful. He and Gull had been the two most talented among us. They were alpha male and alpha female, and of similar age. None of us really knew each other when the team was established, but we all speculated on what might have happened between our two star players.

But the longer we interacted, the more human nature revealed itself.

Xiahou was brilliant, of course, but he couldn't govern his arrogance. He clashed with us often, and his progress with Gull was even more difficult. If she was ever attracted to him, his caustic nature must have ultimately repelled her. Our gossip dwindled as time went on. We gradually got used to conflict, until Gull was buried on Incognita forever, and the planetoid became the object of Xiahou's hatred.

It would have been more appropriate to set aside ego, to conscientiously be the only crystal volunteer, to dedicate oneself to in-depth visual experiments and contribute to the future of science and tech. But if he insisted on hurling himself at Incognita, Team Leader Tian wasn't going to stop him. All she did was pile duty on top of vengeance: Xiahou was to assess whether Incognita was intelligent.

Then Earth would decide whether to deploy weapons. The official countdown had begun.

It took another few weeks—or three lab-grown cell generations—for my research to catch up with Xiahou's progress. I finally understood how the crystal worked, but the direction of that understanding was hard to grasp.

Xiahou must have sensed what was going on. He came to me and we concocted an experiment: he would sit and I would show him various substances in a square glass container.

We had thought there were two protein configurations, that an object occupying space in the visual field triggered the crystal to signal the brain and map the space. But it now appeared we'd been mistaken.

One by one, Xiahou identified the substances I poured in the container, water and alcohol and more, and he identified the empty container. He knew all of this via the optical light path. What the crystal perceived was the phase state of matter. Looking upon the 3D topographical sandbox of the world, he perceived gases ahead that he might pass through. He sensed liquid he might wade through, solids to safely cling to, or annihilating, sterilizing plasma. He could even detect cunning, hidden shear strengths—a trap-detecting sense, a diviner of quicksands and deadly glacial silts.

"In a sense," I said, "instead of calling it depth vision, we might call it touch-at-a-distance."

"Right . . . and Lazeng didn't know what he had. He squandered it. What a waste!"

There he was, the human Xiahou I knew so well: not missing a chance to cast aspersions.

"Or," I said, "his brain was rational enough to defend itself from these powerfully dangerous new functions."

As his departure time drew near, Xiahou began to complain of side effects from touch-at-a-distance. His spatial awareness became too specific. With material composition radically perceived, abstraction became difficult, especially spatial abstraction. This was when he printed the eye patch. From then on, he rarely used his normal right eye. It became increasingly difficult to communicate with him. To him, a small cube and a large one were two qualitatively different things. It was much more convenient for his brain to process data this way. He could verbally summarize either cube, but that was only because some of his cortex was still functioning normally—and he probably understood little or none of this.

He was obsessed with one thing, and he was powerless under its sway. Even Team Leader Tian's orders were merely incidental to him now.

5

My attention returns to the here and now, and to the disposition of *Mad Hunter 2*. Incognita's surface generates countless, unpredictable markings, ephemeral confusions, like a frightened octopus rapidly changing mimicry.

We bear witness to the indestructible, violent will of Incognita itself. To we ordinary mortals, this is a fierce duel, but to one-eyed Xiahou, it could just be a peaceful landing approach.

"Material composition should remain unchanged," Xiahou says. "The changes are optical illusions." His vessel rushes headlong toward the surface, dodging obstacles. Xiahou keeps talking to us, his hands in the control space.

Under his domestication, Incognita finally abandons its transformations and fluctuations. The markings on its surface fade. The visual pressure on us as spectators eases. *Mad Hunter 2* alights safely. Xiahou dons a simulated gravity suit and exits the ship, accompanied by drones.

He sets foot on this strange world.

He treks along ridges, passing crashed spacecraft and entombed alien beasts. Drones record from above and behind the sightseer, transmitting data and analysis back to Earth. Xiahou is always looking around, his field of vision deeper than human, seeking anything anomalous within five kilometers.

"There's a passage through the rock ahead," he announces. "There's an . . . abnormally occupied position . . . at the far end." Xiahou stops in his tracks. "I think that's a skull, human. Can you see it?"

We can all see something like a throne enshrining a skull. These two things seem to be materially integrated. I guess what Xiahou is thinking: the skull might be Gull's.

"Are you sure that's . . . " Team Leader Tian hesitates.

"I have no way of telling if it's real or not . . . no object should be able to exist in so many phases at once."

Xiahou's voice sounds strained. Under his simulated gravity, he trudges forward.

"How far away is it?" Tian says. "I know that's tricky for you, but give us your best guess."

"About a thousand meters," Xiahou says. "I'm proceeding now."

The drones show he is only about three meters from the anomaly, and circling his own position—like a fish circling bait, the line reeling in.

"Don't let it fool you," Tian says.

Xiahou circles closer to the throne. He reaches out and takes the skull, then holds it in his arms. He sits down slowly on the throne. "It's getting darker," he says, pulling the eye patch aside. "I found her, finally. Now I need to rest."

"Let's focus on the mission," Tian says. "Is it conscious? Is Incognita communicating with you?"

We all know our Team Leader is merely trying to keep Xiahou awake, but it's obviously a difficult matter for the explorer to judge:

"Maybe? I can't see anything at the moment. It's bypassing my imaging process, communicating something directly to my brain . . . something beyond logic." He looks up, staring vaguely, blindly, toward a drone camera. I'm shocked by what I see: his left socket no longer contains an eyeball, just an eruption of crystals.

"How do you feel?" I say. "If you can't hold out physically . . . "

"I think I understand now. It's not consciousness connected to my brain, but the world of pure matter. It's matter itself. Incognita doesn't bother with consciousness."

"What do you mean?" Tian says. "An exchange initiated by non-conscious matter?"

"Where do I start?" Xiahou struggles to stand up from the throne. He begins walking toward a nearby mountain range. He scans the peaks with his crystal eye, muttering as he goes:

"In the beginning, a neural network responded to environmental stimuli. Then it grew, eventually becoming so extensive that it needed to form a core. It wasn't willing to passively receive stimuli. It wanted to move, motivated to make predictions about the world it was perceiving. Thus, the brain arose."

Now we can see his destination: a deep cave, a tunnel plunging downward. Such an opening might lead to the core of a planetoid this size.

"Don't go in there!" Tian says.

"Return to *Mad Hunter 2!*" I shout.

Xiahou ignores us, continuing to trudge and conjecture:

"It predicts, gets feedback, self-corrects. By this mechanism, it becomes clever at shielding itself from the vicissitudes of corporeality." He chuckles. "It even takes precautions against the substances that sustain it . . . pure glucose, non-material electrical signals. It's like an emperor hiding behind a screen and never reaching beyond."

We at mission control stand in silent amazement: after all, only by continual retreat can we stop at our place of origin—this is consciousness, desperately protecting itself from nothingness. It seems that the exchange between Incognita and Xiahou was quite efficient. We never imagined anything like this, yet he is able to translate for us, to bring us these surprising truths in forms acceptable by the human brain.

"Are you trying to escape?" Tian asks.

"Escape what?" Xiahou replies.

"Our shields, our human consciousness protections . . . I think you're tempted over there, but I want you to consider it carefully."

"I understand. Humans have evolved consciousness and wisdom at great cost. Of course they'll be unwilling to give them up, but I think I've found something . . . the next filter for the universe, the next level up, or out . . . I guess that explains why Earth is alone in the cosmos. If we don't break through this barrier, we'll never take the next step."

Xiahou's form has vanished into the darkness of the cave. The drones only have a vague infrared ghost of him now.

"But what is forward?" Tian demands. "What is up or out? The pure material world?"

"It's more than that," Xiahou says. "Actually, it's a lively place . . . " The signal relayed by the drones grows weak. "But maybe people aren't ready yet. It takes something like courage, though that word doesn't do it justice. I think I'll take Incognita away, for now."

"You mean you'll let it consume you," I say, but he's already gone.

The slowly revolving planetoid presents the landing site to its sun. *Mad Hunter 2* gleams, and the throne is empty.

Epilogue

Xiahou didn't really "take Incognita away."

We were able to land on it, no longer dazzled or trapped by its defenses, all thanks to Xiahou—but an exhaustive search never turned up his body, or Gull's skull, if it was indeed hers. They were just gone. Ordinarily, with that suit, oxygen and food should have run out. We should have found him dead down there.

Sometimes I recall the story of the dragonfly nymphs. When a dragonfly escapes the water, it becomes something new. There's no turning back. So where did Xiahou fly off to? Maybe he somehow merged with what he called "the world of pure matter."

We've collected minerals and alien remains from Incognita. There are endless secrets to discover. The throne has become a famous landmark on the planetoid, but none of us can communicate with it like Xiahou. We have sealed crystal samples, and it's forbidden to study their fine structures—but they occupy a prominent nexus of our lab complex.

All of us walk by them every day, coming and going, learning and exploring. The samples sit unmoving in their vault. Sometimes it's like they're mocking us in Xiahou's tone:

So, you nymphs think you want to know what's bustling above the water? If you truly want to know, it's actually quite simple. The ultimate chance to leave is here, waiting.

All you have to do is give it a glance.

Originally published in Chinese in *Science Fiction World*, July 2022.

Translated and published in cooperation with *Science Fiction World.*

ABOUT THE AUTHOR

An Hao earned a master's degree in animal science, worked in animal husbandry and genetic engineering, and is a practitioner of Xingyiquan, one of the Chinese Internal Martial Arts. He writes science fiction and ancient Chinese-style fantasy, as well as wuxia. His short story collection *Yes the Spring-Times Needed You Deeply* was published in 2017 and his short story "Yardang Tides" won the 2022 Lenghu Award.

The Fall

JORDAN CHASE-YOUNG

Blue earthshine and bare sunlight soaked the forest of the Moon. The trees stood in silence, white as bone. They, like the animals that dwelled here, had been shaped long ago to survive without atmosphere.

The forest was strange and beautiful, but Chuel feared losing her way in it. Her suit held air for five more hours, enough for her task with some left over. She didn't walk so much as bound, regolith blooming underfoot like short-lived flowers. Some of her crew liked low-g. Found it liberating. To her it felt unnatural, like dreams with dulled physics. She feared having to escape any predators. Though probes had scanned huge swathes of the forest and scholars had wrung knowledge of it from pre-Fall relics, much remained unknown. The Moon had been abandoned for millennia. Who knew what beasts had evolved from the biomodded fauna the Prefalls had left behind?

Happily the animals she'd seen so far were harmless. She photographed them for the settlement's research project. Big white worms and lanky rabbit-frog things. They slithered and hopped away from her but she was quick with the camera, curling her toes with joy whenever she got a good photo.

She clicked through the pics she'd taken, relishing the thought of being the first soul since the Fall to snap the Moon's fauna. If she did nothing else on this mission she'd get her notch in history for that. Probe-pics were trash. The crude robots had beamed nothing of aesthetic value to Earth. But *these* pics. Folk would cite her. Plunk her work in glossy mags. Sure, her crewmates—biologists and archeologists and chemists—would enjoy legacies too. But would anyone other than academics learn their names? Let those eggheads look down on her as a softheaded artist. She'd get the last laugh.

She was scrolling through pics with pride when her eye snagged on something in one. An odd little thing in the regolith. Zooming in, she gasped.

She doubled back and scoured the area, checking and rechecking her camera 'til she found the object. She picked it up, full of wonder. A *doll.* Unimaginably ancient, with willowy limbs and long hair that shifted in low-g as if underwater. A Prefall. Not small and stubby-limbed like modern humans. The outfit was odd. A two-piece affair instead of a jumpsuit.

Chuel smiled sadly, feeling a bond with the owner across time. Whoever they were, they'd been a flesh-and-blood human like her, not just a piece of history. It was easy to forget that.

Wistfully Chuel shook dust off the doll and straightened its hair.

"Been waiting all this time to be found, huh?" Her voice echoed weirdly in her helmet. "Don't worry, little one. You're in good hands now."

She slipped the doll into her suit's free pouch.

She checked her air level and winced. She'd lost track of time.

She set off back toward the settlement, following the steady green blinks of her navigation beacon. She tried not to think about the forest's enormity. It filled her with unease.

An hour later the blinks grew sporadic. She smacked her beacon like an unruly appliance. Some sort of electromagnetic anomaly?

She tried her comm. Nothing.

Panic mushroomed above her diaphragm. Her mission leader Essa had warned her not to lose focus during an assay. *Worryingly susceptible to daydreaming*, her first mission-fitness report had said. Her only red mark. One she'd brought under control well enough to ace her final exam.

If she died out here it was her fault. All that pointless fantasizing about her legacy. Stupid. *Stupid.*

She breathed. A moment's meditation shrank the panic enough for focus.

Three hours of air.

The panic grew past meditation's reach, filling her throat.

If she could get high enough she could spot the settlement. But the trees looked hostile to climbing, their silver leaves agleam like knives. The white wrinkled trunks resembled the poison fungi of her hometown. Could the soft bark even hold her?

She was desperate.

Wrapping her arms around a tree, she climbed like some awkward insect, her vacuprene gloves flensing off rubbery bark in slow cascades.

About thirty meters up, she reached the crown. The boughs underfoot bent easier than any Earth tree's. Even in low-g she doubted they'd keep her weight, but they did. She shimmied to the thickest bough in sight, then climbed to another, fending the urge to look down. A human could fall farther on the Moon than on Earth, but only to a point. The Moon had no air resistance. A fall from this high could be fatal.

She crept to the crown's edge and scanned the canopy. Nothing but silver leaves like a sea of broken solarsheets. But for the rare stirring of animals the canopy was so still it could've been a photo.

She tried her beacon and comm again. Briefly she thought she caught someone's voice, but it was gone.

She checked her air. Regretted it. Shimmied for another view.

She was pushing aside leaves when she sensed movement. A twinge in her periphery.

When she saw the thing it was too late.

A white worm whipped round her throat, knocking her off balance. She tumbled through too-weak branches and plunged from the tree.

As she fell, the worm constricted. She fought it while reaching for her laser. Just as she had the weapon out, she hit ground. Cracks webbed her helmet. A chapel of dust rose, her weapon spinning free and vanishing through it.

The worm's body forked, making lunglike branches that wrestled her down, their sharp whiskers probing her helmet and smearing slime across fractured glass and slicing slowly through the seal.

My legacy, whispered a piece of her. *Dead on the Moon before thirty. No children. No fame. No more picnics behind waterfalls with Thress. Just a stupid pointless death.*

The rest of her was fighting the worm, groping for the laser. Air was hissing through the helmet-cracks.

A beam flared and the worm flashed yellow and was gone, leaving wisps of ash and a single slack strand.

An unfamiliar voice filled her comm. "You okay?"

An astronaut in a strange suit approached, holstering a laser of her own. She helped a stunned Chuel to her feet. Chuel pulled the dead piece of worm off her throat and dropped it. The astronaut was half a meter taller, with long limbs and a shaven head. Her suit like something from an ancient tale. Puffy and cumbersome, not sleek and formfitting like Chuel's.

"You're . . . " *A Prefall*, Chuel wanted to say. Shock tied off her words.

"Nebeth."

"My air's almost gone," Chuel croaked nervously. "And I'm lost."

Nebeth's brown eyes twinkled. "Not anymore. My home's not far."

A warm tide of relief crashed over Chuel. "Thank God. Oh, thank God."

Nebeth led her through the forest in no great hurry. Chuel's astonishment overwhelmed her fear. *A community of Prefalls, still living on the Moon?* There was precedent. A few Denisovans had lingered in New Guinea long after humankind's other cousin species had died. She'd seen a virt on it. But this—this was far more incredible.

"We've been watching your settlement." Nebeth's voice came oddly clear through Chuel's comm.

"I don't understand. Our probes work round the clock, laser-scanning the forest and underground bases. They picked up no activity."

"A place this big, you think your bots will see everything?"

"No, but—"

"Abandon vanity. Don't make our mistake, thinking you know all there is to know."

Nebeth's lack of urgency was frustrating. Chuel's air was falling fast. But she kept her calm. She didn't know Prefall customs and the last thing she wanted was to make Nebeth upset.

"How long have you been watching us?"

"As soon as you arrived," said Nebeth.

"You've made no contact. Why?"

"The others don't want to scare you off."

"You're joking."

"I don't joke."

"*Scare* us? You're—a *treasure*. You're the first Prefall anyone's encountered. We thought you were dead. All of you. This changes *everything*. For humanity. For me. I'll go down in history as the one who found you!"

Nebeth laughed a high cold laugh. "Well, I'm happy for you. What's Earth like these days, anyway?"

"Healing. Slowly. The seas are still underpopulated. But the rainforests are near pre-industrial levels."

"How did you manage that?"

"Most industry's underground now and robots scrub the atmosphere. How much farther?" Chuel thought of blocking the cracks in her helmet with her hand, but she worried the glass would collapse at a touch.

"Almost there," said Nebeth. "It sounds like humans are on a roll. But then so were we."

"We won't screw up again," said Chuel firmly.

Nebeth's tone grew amused. "How can you be sure?"

"I have faith."

"Forgive me for not sharing it."

Chuel couldn't blame her. She couldn't imagine Nebeth's life. Isolated from civilization, convinced it was gone. Only natural she would've fallen into a fatalism so deep even learning humans had recovered couldn't fix it. When Nebeth got back to Earth maybe she would see things different. Maybe.

"We called this forest Grayhaven," said Nebeth. "It was a dry run for terraforming the Solar System. And eventually the Galaxy. But that wasn't our destiny, any more than it's yours. Our destiny was death."

"A destiny's not something you have. It's something you choose."

"That idealism again. You think humankind, in all its squalor and stupidity, will find a way out of the Solar System? There's a reason we've never been visited. Every civilization's on the clock. Just how it is."

Nebeth's words grated so much that for a moment Chuel didn't even care about her air levels. "That's crazy. If we made it this far there's no limit to what we can do. Neither of us would be here if our ancestors saw things like you."

"No. They'd know better than to waste their lives on dead ends. If they had common sense they would've spent more time protecting their gifts—family and nature and community—and less on feats of hubris."

The airlock loomed between trees like an ancient tomb, all harsh edges and crude paneling. Attached was the elevator turret leading to a sublunar colony.

Finally.

Nebeth was cycling the airlock when Chuel's comm crackled.

"Hello?" Chuel called. "Can you hear me?"

No reply.

"Strange interference around here," said Nebeth. "We'll find your crew. First need to get you out of that busted suit."

Nebeth took Chuel by the arm.

The comm spat again. A man's voice, garbled. The chief medic. "Chuel!"

"Ivyn?"

"Chuel, are you . . . ?"

"I'm here! Here!" Silence. "*Hello?*"

Nebeth's face gained a shade of displeasure. "I said we'll find your crew after."

"They're close, I have to reach them."

Nebeth's grip tightened, her big gloves squeezing Chuel's vacuprene.

Chuel tried to pull away but Nebeth wouldn't let go. The Prefall tried to drag Chuel into the airlock.

"Stop. Wait. *Please.*"

"Pointless to fight your destiny." As Nebeth's head passed the airlock's threshold her eyes dwindled like smoke from their sockets and her hair tumbled from a peeling scalp like dead moss. Her suit faded and frayed and deflated about her bones like some ancient parachute coming to rest on a knobbled armature. Her voice shrived to a rasp. "You're almost there."

Chuel screamed. She pulled from Nebeth with all her strength and broke free and fell backward into blooming regolith.

Chuel's comm exploded with Nebeth's rage and hurt, a sound of envy and despair so sharp it pinned Chuel to the ground like a knife. Chuel screwed her eyes shut and ground her teeth and when the sound slowly ceased she opened her eyes again, blinking through sun glare. But it wasn't the sun. And she wasn't where she was supposed to be. The airlock was gone. She was back beside the tree she'd fallen from. A man was kneeling beside her, flitting a medical light across her eyes. Ivyn.

Essa, the mission leader, was slicing something white off Chuel's throat with a heat-knife. A stubborn remnant of the worm.

"She's concussed," said Ivyn. "Can you hear me, Chuel?"

Chuel could only nod.

"Thank God," said Essa.

"She's hurt bad." Ivyn was pumping air into Chuel's suit through a nozzle. "Organ bruising, probably."

Essa shook her head. "Lucky she shot the worm or we'd be hauling a corpse home. Damn thing almost cut through the casing."

Shot the worm? But . . . Chuel saw that she was clutching her laser.

She felt memories slipping from her like a dream after waking. But it hadn't been a dream. She knew—knew in her bones—that she'd met *something*. Something sad and lonely and angry. And very real.

All she remembered were words. Words like *destiny* and *death*. They tumbled through her skull as she looked at Earth above Essa's shoulder, shining weak through white branches and silver leaves.

"What's this?" Essa pulled the doll from Chuel's pouch. The little Prefall, its head lolling from a broken neck. Essa wondered at it.

If Chuel had any strength she would've thrown the doll back into the shadows of the forest. But she could only stare at it, chilled by a nameless fear.

ABOUT THE AUTHOR

Oregon's gray skies stamped **Jordan Chase-Young** into a science-fiction writer. Now he lives in Australia with his wife Caitie and their psycho-cat Hilda. When he's not working or puzzling over the fate of his starbent species through prose, he's drawing strange creatures or strolling Melbourne's sunny streets for inspiration. His stories have appeared or are forthcoming in *Escape Pod, The Magazine of Fantasy & Science Fiction,* the Zombies Need Brains anthology *When Worlds Collide,* and many other venues. He occasionally blogs about the future at E-Book of the New Sun.

Horror and Science Fiction: Genre's Evil Twins

CARRIE SESSAREGO

Science fiction and horror are like siblings who sometimes quarrel, and sometimes live separate lives, but always come back together. Defining genre always leads to controversy, but one might say that science fiction asks, "Wouldn't it be exciting if X were true?" and horror asks, "Wouldn't it be terrifying if X were true?"

Science fiction and horror are both driven by curiosity, but their different attitudes towards curiosity create a special tension when the genres merge. In science fiction, curiosity can be a wonderful thing. In this case, the answer to "What if?" leads to remarkable discoveries. The original Star Trek series, while it had many brushes with horror ("A Wolf in the Fold," for instance) was based on the belief that positive answers to "What if?" were in abundance. Despite some scary and some tragic episodes, *Star Trek* was driven by the belief that a mission to "explore strange new worlds. To seek out new life and new civilizations. To boldly go where no man has gone before!" would lead to a generally improved quality of life for humanity. Curiosity was seen as a positive trait that would usually be rewarded.

In horror, curiosity not only kills the cat, but it also reanimates and turns them into a killing machine. The primal sin in horror is to be curious. While science fiction says "Boldly go! Check out that new life form! Make friends with that new civilization," horror tells us "Stay at home! Do not open that weird puzzle box, do not investigate that noise, and above all do not respond to that distress call!" Yet, without curiosity in horror there can be no catharsis, just as without curiosity in science fiction there can be no discovery. In both genres, curiosity exposes the truth, exposing secrets and opening the way for a new reality, whether desirable or not.

Science fiction and horror have been linked since the birth of the science fiction genre. The very first modern science fiction novel, *Frankenstein*, is also a horror novel. *Frankenstein* asks the question, "What would happen if a scientist were able to finesse the newly discovered power of electricity, as well as other non-supernatural means, to create life from death?" It is horror because the answer is "Nothing good." Earlier horror stories invoked the supernatural and fear of the supernatural, but everything that happens in *Frankenstein* is presumably explained by Victor Frankenstein's mechanical and scientific process and by the workings of hubris and loss, envy and rage that result in his creating a person and then abandoning them to a fearful world.

Frankenstein's particular anxiety is connected in a straight and bloody line to other stories of scientific hubris, absence of accountability, and unforeseen consequences, especially those that involve creating life through artificial means. Stories about AI gone rogue, such as *Ex Machina* (2014) and "I Have No Mouth and I Must Scream" (Harlan Ellison, 1967), are at once science fiction thought experiments and exercises in horror. Meanwhile the Jurassic Park franchise features scientists creating dinosaurs who promptly eat a lot of people. A famous line from *Jurassic Park* (1993), "Your scientists were so preoccupied with whether or not they could, that they didn't stop to think if they should," could apply just as easily to *Frankenstein* as to any number of other science fiction horror movies and novels in which "life finds a way," usually by bloodily devouring other life.

Arguably the other biggest classical influence on science fiction horror comes from H.P. Lovecraft (with a nod to H.G. Wells, whose *Island of Doctor Moreau* and *War of the Worlds* combined science fiction and horror to iconic effect). While some of H.P. Lovecraft's work is specifically supernatural in nature, much of his work toggles the line between supernatural horror and science fiction horror. "The Color Out of Space" is a famous example of one of his stories that uses science fiction and horror together to great effect. The horrible things that happen in the story are the result of a meteorite that falls to Earth, bringing with it a color never seen before and a host of lethal side effects. Lovecraft wanted to create something that would be truly alien, and he succeeded, as the color cannot be communicated with or understood by any means at our disposal. Is it a living being? Does it wreak havoc on purpose? Is it conscious? Is it a kind of animal, or more of a virus, or maybe a fungus? The color's very existence is so beyond the realms of human science that it feels like something supernatural, and yet the terror of it comes partly from the fact that it is implied to be a natural phenomenon—just one that humanity has never before encountered. It is natural; therefore, we may encounter it again. But it is also unknowable, therefore we will not be able to survive an encounter.

In stories like these, Lovecraft used science fiction concepts of alien life to explore the existential horror of humanity's insignificance in a vast and unknowable universe. Technically, the cosmic entities in his stories (most famously, Cthulhu) can be considered to be aliens, but these alien lifeforms are so far beyond the comprehension of humans that they are, for all intents and purposes, supernatural, and that tension between what we can comprehend and what we cannot is what breaks the minds of Lovecraft's characters.

Optimistic science fiction stories treat the vastness of space with curiosity and excitement. Lovecraft stories operate by demonstrating how very vast, and how very powerless, we are in this universe. In Lovecraftian horror, scientists, scholars, and people who just happen to be in the wrong place at the wrong time express curiosity about the universe, but the answers are so inexplicable as to drive most of the characters insane. His scientists want to follow the science fiction precept of exploration, but when they do they run headlong into a horror construct of badness.

The definition of science fiction is under constant debate, but it seems generally accepted by the public that science fiction takes place in the future, even if the future is the very near future (sometimes described as 'Five Minutes From Now'). The central question of science fiction, its Prime Directive, if you will, is to engage the curiosity of the reader or the viewer and ask "What would happen if?" What would happen if we discovered that we lived in an artificial reality (*The Matrix* (1999), *Dark City* (1998)? What would happen if we set up a colony on Mars (*The Mars Trilogy* by Kim Stanley Robinson, *The Martian Chronicles* by Ray Bradbury)? What if there was a language we could use to defeat our interstellar enemies (*Babel-17* by Samuel R. Delany)?

Horror, meanwhile, must frighten the viewer or reader. This is horror's Prime Directive. Although *E.T.: The Extraterrestrial* (1982) has many frightening sequences, its primary goal is not to terrify the viewer. Rather, its primary purpose is to touch us emotionally with the unbreakable bond between a little boy and an alien being. *Cloverfield* (2008), on the other hand, does not want you to leave the movie with a nuanced sense of what communicating with an alien might be like.

It wants to scare the pants off you. When the answer to "What if?" is "A bunch of scary stuff!", then we have science fiction horror.

Looking at stories from different genre lenses can deepen our understanding of the story by exposing aspects of its questions, motifs, and structures that we may previously have ignored. *Alien* (1979) and *The Terminator* (1984) are both undeniably science fiction, but they are also quite traditional slasher movies, combining the themes and imagery of science fiction with the structure and rules of horror films, specifically slasher films. The push/pull between the science fiction story and the horror structure adds to the tension of the work, especially since the audience can't be sure which genre's rules will apply.

Both genres include an enormous variety of storytelling styles and attitudes. Space exploration horror such as the found footage movie *The Europa Report* (2013) suggests that instead of seeking out new worlds, we had probably better just stay on Earth. Monster stories, alien invasion stories, and AI Gone Wrong stories are various branches from the dual tree of *Frankenstein* by way of unintended consequences of human activity (experimentation, pollution, and use of nuclear weapons for instance) and by way of Lovecraft (our insignificance in an unknowable world). Stories can be driven by, or include, body horror, disease-driven horror, isolation horror, or any combination thereof. These are only a few of the myriad subgenres, many of which often overlap.

One commonality between horror and science fiction is that they both adhere to certain rules. It is these rules, this sense of structure, that allows for a sense of satisfying catharsis. In science fiction, there must always be an explanation for events that is not supernatural. While other sub-genres of horror are free to invoke the supernatural and very often do, meldings of these genres must include at least one plausible mundane explanation for events. *M3GAN* (2022) is a "scary doll" story in which the doll is a robot, which provides a technical and mundane explanation for her strength, intelligence, and homicidal tendencies. Thus, M3GAN belongs in the ranks of science fiction horror. Another creepy doll, Chucky from *Child's Play* (1988), is given his powers through magic, which places him firmly in the ranks of supernatural horror.

Science fiction, with its forward gazing lens, rewards the reader or viewer for curiosity, exploration, heroism, even, in many stories, unorthodox expressions of gender and sexuality as well as drug use. Horror, on the other hand, has been described by Stephen King as "innately conservative, even reactionary" in the sense that the genre provides relief from tension when the plot "re-establishes our feelings of essential normality." The rules of slasher movies in particular have been articulated in *Scream* (1996): "You can never have sex . . . You can never drink or do drugs. The sin factor! It's a sin. It's an extension of number one. And number three: never, ever, ever under any circumstances say, 'I'll be right back.' Because you won't be back."

In science fiction, catharsis arrives when science saves the day. In horror, catharsis arrives in a variety of ways, but the primary catharsis comes from the viewer or reader experiencing a scary situation in a safe way—practice, in an emotional sense, for handling fear in unsafe situations. These two kinds of catharsis create a new tension in science fiction horror, because science might NOT save the day, and following the rules of horror might NOT save the characters—indeed, things that we thought would be scientifically explained might be left mysterious. The same things that we are rewarded for in one genre can doom us in another, and it's anyone's guess who will win out.

Consider, for instance, the decisions characters make in *Alien*. In a straight science fiction film, surely our crew would be rewarded for their heroism in responding to a distress call, their curiosity about the alien ship, and their refusal to leave a crew member behind. Instead, the more heroic and curious the crew behaves, the more doomed they become. At the same time, the science fiction setting allows for stunning ideas, imagery, and implications that would not be possible in a horror movie set in the present.

Another way that we see science fiction and horror interacting is in their use of imaginary situations to discuss real-world taboos. Science fiction and horror, like their cousins mystery and romance, are genres that play in metaphor, and this use of metaphor and allegory gives them the ability to take chances and express topics that 'literary fiction' cannot. By invoking futuristic and/or supernatural metaphors, these genres can discuss issues with some plausible deniability. For instance, at a time when mixed-race relationships were widely vilified, *Star Trek* explored these relationships and the children of these relationships sympathetically through the lens of Spock, the science officer who has a father from the planet Vulcan and a human mother. Later on, *Star Trek: Deep Space Nine* used the concept of an alien symbiote species to explore questions of gender and sexuality. While using alien races as stand-ins for marginalized humans is deeply problematic, it is the structure of science fiction that allowed them to be discussed at all in a mainstream forum at the time.

Even when topics are discussed in mainstream media, using science fiction and horror allows us to look at them differently. The lenses of genre can help us see different experiences and viewpoints from fresh angles. For instance, writer/director/producer Jordan Peele uses science fiction and horror in his movies *Get Out, Us,* and *Nope* to explore different aspects of Black life and socio-economic and racial politics. These movies center Black lives and viewpoints, making them the heroes of the story and using allegory and metaphor to illustrate the surreal and horrific experiences that Black people in America often experience in ways that cut through topical arguments.

One reason that *Frankenstein* has had so many adaptations in so many different kinds of media is that the storyline allows for so many difficult topics to be addressed. Mary Shelley wrote the book partly inspired by her own experiences with parental abandonment. The concept of the scientist creating new life allows for conversations about gender roles, about technology, about hubris, about the role of science in daily life, about exploration, and about empathy. These concepts are not unique to *Frankenstein* or to science fiction horror by any means, but science fiction horror gives us a unique venue in which to have these conversations because talking about issues through metaphor and allegory is sometimes both easier and more illuminating than sitting down to a conversation about reproductive rights, or deadbeat dads, or GMO's, even though those head-on conversations are important ones to have.

Meanwhile, the very lack of respectability that the horror genre possesses allows it to violate taboos and accepted storytelling limits. When combined with the futuristic gaze of science fiction, horror can be as gross as *Human Centipede* (2009), as weird as *Annihilation* (2019), as shocking as *Event Horizon* (1997). The push/pull between the "anything can happen" of science fiction and "any line can be crossed as long as it is scary" of horror creates fertile ground for controversial material. While the world arguably could have existed just fine without *Human Centipede*, the fact remains that many of the world's most beloved art works were panned as being too transgressive upon their release and only reassessed by later generations. Whether they are awful or sublime, transgressive stories in any media are important in pushing audiences to consider what our limits are and why, and whether, they should exist.

While science fiction can be deeply personal and horror can be abstract, they usually operate on different planes that, when they interact, create a balance between thought and feeling. Science fiction generally presents itself as a thought experiment. The characters may be richly drawn, the story moving, the plot thrilling, but the premise, the core of the story, is an idea, an intellectual exercise. If this idea does not interest the viewer or reader, the whole thing falls apart.

Horror, on the other hand, is all about emotion. The concepts may be massive in scope, but horror only works if it engages emotion. It is personal, enacted upon the bodies of the characters and activating a whole stew of chemicals in the brain of the reader or viewer. Yes, there are a lot of theological implications to the idea of demon possession in *The Exorcist* (1973), but the core of the story is the trauma visited upon the body of poor little Regan and the fight, flight, or freeze instincts of the viewer. If the emotions of fear are not experienced by the viewer, the whole thing falls apart.

Not all horror is science fiction and vice versa, and not all science fiction horror is good. However, at its best, the worlds of idea and emotion, the tension between curiosity as a positive and a negative quality, and the upheaval of expectations, creates a new and potent mix. Like the monster in *Frankenstein*, it becomes something more than the sum of its parts. It turns out that while, "In Space, no one can hear you scream," it's a very good place to do it.

ABOUT THE AUTHOR

Carrie Sessarego is the resident "geek reviewer" for *Smart Bitches, Trashy Books,* where she wrangles science fiction, fantasy romance, comics, movies, and non-fiction. Carrie's first book, *Pride, Prejudice, and Popcorn: TV and Film Adaptations of Pride and Prejudice, Wuthering Heights, and Jane Eyre,* was released in 2014. Her work has been published in *Interfictions Online, Pop Matters: After the Avengers, The WisCon Chronicles Vol. 9, Invisible 3, Clarkesworld Magazine,* and two volumes of *Speculative Fiction: The Year's Best Online Reviews, Essays and Commentary.* She spends her time wrangling her husband, daughter, dog, and three cats.

Gods Aren't Necessarily Nice: A Conversation with Premee Mohamed

ARLEY SORG

Premee Mohamed was born in Edmonton, Alberta, Canada. She lived in Calgary for about two years for work/a university co-op term, and Saskatoon, Saskatchewan for a university co-op term, but ultimately moved back to Edmonton for work. She earned two BScs from the University of Alberta, one after high school, the other after working for a while. "Growing up, I wanted to do primary research, but then I did do that for a while after graduating from the genetics degree and decided that I wanted to do something else, maybe with a field work component, so environmental science appealed to me."

Writing has been a part of Mohamed's life for a long time—as a fun hobby, something she hadn't planned to take seriously. According to family legend, Mohamed taught herself to read around age two. "My parents are sticking to that story! They're literally like, 'We never bothered reading to you, because you were doing it for yourself.' " An anecdote about a childhood school project reveals a lot about Mohamed's vision for herself: "Mom found a 'book' I wrote in Grade 9 (1995, I think?), when one of our class projects was for everyone in the class to write and bind a book, which was really fun. It's not a book-book, more short story length. But the little 'author bio' on the back says that I'm thirteen, and I would like to be an oncologist when I grow up. (The book was about a kid who does stage magic and performs what seems to be an impossible trick, and becomes exploited by an evil manager and then has to escape him.)"

For Mohamed, writing was a private activity. She didn't share it with people in general and had no intention to publish. She wrote to relax. "I really only got into publishing because a friend was bugging me to submit a short story to an anthology call that he was like, 'This is the kind of stuff you read, isn't it?', because we had been talking about the books we were reading at the time." The editors—Silvia Moreno-Garcia and Paula R. Stiles—accepted the story, "The Adventurer's Wife", and the anthology happened to be *She Walks in Shadows*, published by Innsmouth Free Press in 2015, which went on to win a World Fantasy Award.

"So, I started submitting short stories for pocket money, because I was writing anyway!" Mohamed followed up with magazine appearances: "The Last" in *Metaphorosis* and "The Honeymakers" in *Syntax & Salt*, both in 2016. In 2017 she had nine short stories published across a variety of magazines and anthologies, including notable venues like *Mythic Delirium*, *Shoreline of Infinity*, and the Escape Artists horror venue *PseudoPod*. To-date, she has over forty stories out, including 2018 self-published novella *The Apple-Tree Throne*, and 2021 novellas *These Lifeless Things* (Solaris), *And What Can We Offer You Tonight* (Neon Hemlock), and *The Annual Migration of Clouds* (ECW).

Mohamed's longer-form work began with 2020 debut novel *Beneath the Rising* (Solaris), which was an Aurora, British Fantasy, Locus, and Crawford Award finalist. Sequel *A Broken Darkness* followed in 2021, which was also a finalist for Locus, British Fantasy, and Aurora Awards. Book Three, *The Void Ascendant*, came out in 2022. But her novels were not her only works to earn acclaim. *These Lifeless Things* was an Aurora and British Fantasy Award finalist; *The Annual Migration of Clouds* was an Aurora winner, plus a Robert Kroetsch City of Edmonton Book Prize finalist and a Georges Bugnet Award for Fiction finalist; *And What Can We Offer You Tonight* won a Nebula and a World Fantasy Award. Mohamed has also received grants from the Alberta Foundation for the Arts, the Edmonton Arts Council, and the Marian Hebb Research Program.

Mohamed does feel the draw of other cities, especially places like Vancouver and Montreal, where many of her friends live. But she feels that Alberta has its advantages: "On the plus side the cost of living is more reasonable here and this might be one of the only large-ish (million-plus population) cities in the country where someone can buy a house on a single income." And, despite her accolades, including a recent career milestone of being flown-in as a guest to Halifax SFF convention HalCon, she doesn't see writing as a career endgame. "Full-time writer is never going to be a thing for me because I'm barely making any money from book sales, certainly not enough to cover bills, so I don't even consider it an option . . . I just spent almost a decade working in environmental policy and I'd like to stay in the environmental field—maybe something related to climate change and clean tech, or ecosystem restoration."

Mohamed has two novellas with ECW Press in the works, both are sequels to *The Annual Migration of Clouds*; as well as a novella with Tordotcom called *The Butcher of the Forest*. More immediately, Mohamed's debut collection is due from Undertow this month: *No One Will Come Back for Us*.

Who do you see as your literary heroes (or: what are the works that have been important to you), and what do you love most about their work?

Every time I think about this, I think the list is different! I keep wondering whether 'literary hero' means that I want to write like them, or it means I want to be like them (as a person), or whether it means I want a career like theirs. I love Nick Harkaway's writing and the way his books are constantly zigging and zagging against expectations; I love Gene Wolfe's prose and the fact that he helped invent the machine that shapes Pringles; I love the complex, layered worldbuilding in Ursula K. Le Guin's books (ideas, setting, character, values, politics, religion, geography, wildlife, technology, everything so carefully considered and working together); I love William Faulkner's and Umberto Eco's use of language and voice.

Most recently, I've started reading all of John Crowley's stuff, thinking it would all be like *Ka* and *Little, Big*, and instead I'm delighted by how different the writing is in each book, depending on the premise and the subject. That's so important to me, as someone who isn't wild about writing the same book again and again. Also, after John le Carre's death, I decided to start reading his books in publication order and I'm deeply impressed by the clever characterization and plot twists, and his use of vivid, unexpected metaphors. I'm constantly highlighting individual sentences like "Oh my God, I never would have thought of that, I love it."

For you, what is the impact of being a scientist on the way you engage with genre? Do you prefer reading stories with more rigorous scientific accuracy? And does this mean your own fiction tends to be more rigorous as well?

This is such a good question, and the answer keeps evolving! It certainly means I'm a little more sensitive to stories where the fundamental premise strikes me as either unscientific or anti-scientific . . . I see the occasional thread of anti-intellectualism or anti-science rhetoric that really rubs me the wrong way. But in terms of overall reading preferences, I'm okay if the scientific accuracy in the book isn't entirely there, provided it's handwaved in a way that I enjoy.

I'm not going to jump onto Reddit and start harping about how "WELL, THAT'S NOT HOW IT WORKS" unless it's something so obvious that it "broke" the book for me and ruined my suspension of disbelief. This often happens when people overexplain (and get things wrong) rather than underexplain. It's okay to just say "We cloned Steve" and move on with the scene, I promise! Because if you tell a geneticist *how* you cloned Steve and it's *ridiculous*, I may get annoyed and stop reading!

It's just the occasional thing that jumps out at me that'll make me throw a book across the room—where it's blatantly affecting the plot, or someone clearly didn't do just thirty seconds of research, or it's common-sense stuff (like I was flailing and struggling to leave the theater in the first G.I. Joe movie where they blow up something and the ice below it starts sinking to the bottom of the ocean, and my friends—I was there with a couple of engineers—were pinning me in my seat like "We *know* it's stupid, we *know* ice floats, but the movie is almost over"). It's not necessarily a deal-breaker, but it occasionally can be. Or I was just reading something where the author referred to a bunch of fragrant plants growing in a rich person's garden and they talk about "the scent of saffron coming from the saffron tree" and like . . .

two seconds of research would have told you that saffron comes from a flower, not a tree.

I think the biggest impact of having a scientific background is not related to my particular areas of expertise but how I research—not just what sources I use and what I pick out of them, but also how I organize what I find and how I string it together when I want to turn it into fiction. If I know a lot about a particular subject, I know how I can twist or tweak it in a story so that the reader can understand it, so that it's interesting, so that it's useful to the narrative, but also so that the 5% of what I talk about in the story doesn't contradict the 95% of the research that didn't go in there. Things connect to each other in strange ways no matter what you're researching once you've looked up enough papers about it, and I love it when that happens. That's exactly how my stories tend to come together: a zillion disparate things that somehow join up and form a pattern.

You have a slew of short stories out, as well as novella-length pieces. Is your relationship to short fiction very different from your relationship to novella or novel length work?

Definitely very, very different! I find short stories incredibly difficult to write. The shorter they are, the harder they are for me. I had to write a <500 word one for a local magazine a while back and there was like a six-month lead time on it and I was like "Thank God, I'm going to *need* the whole six months." My natural length is novel or novella. It's hard for me to look at an idea and say, "That's something I'd like to explore in 4000 words," and not instinctively spin off all the related ideas into a full-length book. Novels and novellas are where I feel like I can stretch, be comfortable, not feel cramped or limited, go off on tangents, let things grow and progress slowly (characters, situations, disasters), build things bit by bit. I always feel like I'm fretting and chafing at the word count limitation in a short story; I am definitely not a "natural" short fiction author.

I love being solicited for things where the editor gives me a theme or a piece of source material as well as the word count, because that helps me wrestle my out-of-control ideas into a box where I can sift through them for something relevant that will actually fit what they need. Right now, it's pretty rare that I'm writing a short story "just for me" to send out on submission. It just fries all the brain cells I need for writing novels and novellas and solicited shorts.

Your debut novel came out in 2020 but you had written it considerably earlier. What was "breaking in" for you, what was the process like and how did it happen?

Yes, I finished *Beneath the Rising* in 2002 and set it aside; when I decided to start querying to seek out a literary agent, that one got picked not because I thought it was any good, but because it was done (I have a huge trunk full of discarded stuff, but the main problem is that 90% of the stuff is incomplete. Some of it is unbelievably long, but . . . still not done). I gave it a light polish and sent it out to agents, and ended up getting two offers of representation. I went with my current agent (Michael Curry) because he also represents Cassandra Khaw and Nick Mamatas, so I was like "Okay, at a bare minimum I know he likes modern cosmic horror and can sell it."

Beneath the Rising was on submission for a long time and got a lot of lovely rejections, like, "We loved this, but we can't take it to acquisitions because it's too amorphously placed between sci-fi, fantasy, and horror." I was actually pleased when Solaris picked it up, because they were open to stuff that lands between genres. (Yoon Ha Lee's wonderful Machineries of Empire series comes to mind). They bought it in a two-book deal, so I wrote a sequel, and then shortly before book two came out, they approached us for a book three—which took some fancy footwork because I had worked so hard to tie off all the threads and close all the doors at the end of what I assumed was going to be a duology. It seems to have worked out though!

In terms of "breaking out" I'm not sure that's what's happened here; by the end of 2024 I will have eleven books out with six different publishers, so it's not really a case of "getting in" with a regular publisher or an editor who wanted to invest in and develop my career. I'm more like a traveling salesman with a suitcase full of books to sell to whatever friendly person opens the door. I wouldn't call it a publishing career even at this point; it's still just a hobby (and paying like a hobby). Honestly, at this point, it's looking like I'll have to hand in my next couple of contracted books and drop out of sight entirely, because I physically can't manage working and publishing at the same time. I might be able to manage working and *writing* again if my health improves, but as they say, "Watch out for that last step, it's a lulu" when the last step is publishing.

How did you get into dark fiction and horror? Was there a gateway, or was it just always a part of your reading habit?

I've always loved dark fiction and horror. Some of the earliest stuff I can remember loving was from these big anthologies I picked up cheap at a library sale—they had a weird basementy smell and slightly smudgy black and white illustrations. There was a collected Edgar Allan Poe, a Robert E. Howard one, and my favorite, an Edgar Rice Burroughs one (the illustrations were also the clearest in that one). I loved the danger and adventure in the Conan stories and the Barsoom stories.

My parents didn't much care what I read provided that my grades were okay; they generally didn't check what I was bringing home from the library, for example. And at school I could read whatever I wanted. I probably got into Stephen King a little too early (I read *It* when I was about the same age as the kids in the Losers Club) but what I really wanted was stuff more like Poe and Howard: fantasy horror, monsters and adventure, swords and sorcery and dark lords and wizards. Contemporary horror often grossed me out but didn't scare me.

I definitely wanted to be scared, and specifically by something like Sauron in The Lord of the Rings or Arawn in *The Book of Three*. Funnily enough, I didn't get into cosmic horror until I was in my twenties, when I read some Lovecraft short stories in university and then started looking up related writers after I went through all his stuff. I was never a fan of horror movies though; they didn't scratch the right itch I was looking for in terms of scares.

What is it about dark fiction and horror that is important or special—how does it work, or what does it do, that other modes of writing don't quite accomplish?

Good question, and I'm still feeling my way towards an answer, I think . . . I have a lot of friends in this space who can answer this better than me, but I think there's an *honesty* in horror, in horror elements, that forms a fundamental part of the narrative. A character in a horror novel has to dig deep, confront their own limitations, flaws, delusions, prejudices, and assumptions in a way that the plot doesn't force you to do in most other genres.

In a horror book, what's after you is probably inexorable. Maybe you can fight it, maybe you can't. You certainly don't believe you can defeat it for most of the book. Maybe you don't have any help—maybe people don't even *believe* you. Nothing in the plot is coming to rescue you; other characters don't want to be exposed to the horror either. All the comforting layers of what makes us safe are stripped away.

Horror lets you, the reader, feel the movie camera on you, watching you: What are you going to do now? Are you scared? Are you admitting you're scared? As you read about what's happening to these characters, do you feel something inside yourself? Will you allow yourself to say what you feel? What I love about horror is that the discomfort is the point. The camera won't swivel away at the last minute. It'll make you look.

Your debut collection, No One Will Come Back For Us, features a 2015 story "The Adventurer's Wife", but the book also offers newer pieces such as 2020 story "The Redoubtables" and the 2021 story "Everything as Part of Its Infinite Place". Looking at this range of work, do you see specific ways in which your writing has changed?

I do, I think! That first story ("The Adventurer's Wife") is such a Lovecraft pastiche that it makes me cringe. It's barely even imitative; it's like someone fed a bunch of his short stories into a machine-learning bot and it spit out this story. One thing I used to do, without realizing quite how bad it was, was getting way too limited and literal with a given theme. Like, for a Lovecraft anthology, I wouldn't initially think of doing something actually interesting or modern, like a retelling, or studying and subverting the tropes; I literally just wrote something Lovecraft would have written. (In my defense, it was the first short story I'd written since I was thirteen or fourteen years old!)

As time went on, I started reading a lot more modern short fiction, not like the short stories I'd read in school (all the usual suspects in Norton anthologies) and seeing what people were doing now in terms of voice and format and structure and style. It was like that moment in *The Wizard of Oz* where things turn to color: What? You can do all this in short fiction? You can do whatever you want?! Yes, you can absolutely do whatever you want, there are no Short Story Police out there waiting to pull you over for not writing something that looks exactly like some story from 1913.

So "The Redoubtables" was written for *Apparition Lit*'s "experimentation" call and I played with that in two ways: it's about an experimental weapon, and since it's structured as a nonfiction essay being written by a young journalist, it's also an experiment in form. I've been letting myself get more adventurous with short fiction as time has gone on (or, again, maybe just getting bolder as I continue to evade arrest by the Short Story Police). "The Youngest Son Misses His Boat to the Crusades" (*Tales & Feathers*) barely has a plot and is written in repetitive, poetic language; "More Tomorrow" (*Automata Magazine*) is written as a series of incomplete journal entries; "The Trick Question" (*99 Tiny Terrors*) was based on a Rilke poem. I still write a lot of stories that I feel are Shaped Like A Short Story, but there's so much else out there to explore and I'm actively trying to explore it, albeit at a slow pace.

How were stories selected for the collection? Is there an organizational principle at work, is it thematic, or do you see it as a "best of" bringing together your finest work to-date?

My editor, Michael Kelly, contacted me and my agent and specifically asked if he could have a selection that was "dark fantasy and horror." When I pressed (because I loved "The Redoubtables" and desperately wanted it to go with the others) he said it was also OK to have sci-fi, provided it was also dark and not strictly sci-fi-y sci-fi. Nothing too whimsical, nothing with a super happy ending (though I think "Instructions" is actually very silly). My agent and I joked that it shouldn't be too hard to find a few hopeless or ambiguous endings in my stuff!

Basically, I went through and picked out the stories I thought fit Michael's brief, plus one unpublished one ("Quietus") that had been acquired for an anthology and even edited, but then the anthology didn't happen. I sent them in chronological order and let Michael choose the order; all I asked was that "Quietus" come last because I loved the ending and wanted that to be the ending for the whole collection, and that "Us & Ours" came after "The Evaluator" because while the stories are happening at about the same time, one story sets up the world and helps provide context for the second one. So the final order for the collection is what Michael came up with and it works for me! I don't think it's a best-of, nor was it meant to be; I think if I were picking my own best-of it would include stories from this collection, but also others. This collection is more in alignment with Undertow's editorial vision of dark, weird horror, so that's what we stuck to.

What can you tell us about the original story, "Quietus", without "spoiling" the read too much?

"Quietus" came out of some research I was doing about unihemispherical sleep, which is something some animals can do (basically, they're awake and asleep at the same time, so they can rest while still being alert to threats) but humans, as far as studies have shown, can't. In the story, it's split between following a group of military scientists as they attempt to induce unihemispherical sleep in their test subject, and the test subject himself, who sees himself fighting in endless historical wars while the scientists manipulate his brain. But, scientists being scientists, one of them simply wants to go too far. This is probably the most research I've ever done for a short story, but a) it was all interesting and b) I had a lot of fun turning it into fiction.

Thinking about these stories gathered in this book, are there ideas, themes, or concerns that you feel like you often tend to come back to? Or does your work vary greatly from piece to piece, approaching a range of concerns?

Good question! I really had to go back and look. I think I definitely come back to themes and tropes from cosmic horror a lot, even in stories that don't seem to be about it ("Everything As Part of Its Infinite Place" comes to mind). Just this idea that the enemy ranged against you isn't always identifiable as an enemy; you might just be in the wrong place in the wrong time in a random universe. Plus the idea that you might think you know someone, but you don't truly know them till they're afraid.

"Gods aren't necessarily nice" is also a common theme in here. I grew up with a Hindu mother and a Muslim father who didn't attend services or participate in their religious community or traditions; I also spent about twelve years in Catholic school without having been baptized or anything. So I was always surrounded by religion but never belief, if that makes any sense. I'm very interested in belief and faith: what do people feel, what does it feel like, how do they feel about their place in the universe, does it make a difference if you can sometimes see the gods or if they show up at your house.

I also am struck by how many of these very dark stories feature children and difficult parental relationships that are integral to the horror. I don't have kids and have never wanted kids, but I think it's fascinating to see kids in horror stories playing various roles: innocent victims, as wily escapees from victimhood, as willing participants in the horror, as unwilling participants, as part of a trade or deal, as survivors, as villains, as observers. We think of children as these innocent, unknowing beings that we need to protect and shelter—but kids are watching all the time, it's how they learn, they're aware of a lot more than we give them credit for, because we remember our own childhoods differently as we get older.

I think the main theme in all my stories though is that for a lot of us, what we *really want* is to change the world; why is that, and why do so many of us fall apart when we realize that's never going to happen and the world is going to change us instead?

Which of the stories in the collection, for you, were most challenging to write? What made them challenging, and how did you face those challenges?

I think in terms of amount of research, "Quietus" was the most challenging, but actually sitting down and writing the story and having it look the way it did in my head, that felt no worse than any other story. "The General's Turn" was torture because the original was over 13,000 words, so I had to cut and cut and cut and it took forever. There was just so much more world (and more war and more evil and more tradition) to discuss and I hated having to snip it out in order to keep even the slightest bit of narrative momentum in, when you look at it, kind of a minimal plot.

But in this collection, I think "The Redoubtables" went through the most frustrating false starts: I initially wrote it from the POV of a scientist on the island, then from someone working with the Consortium, then from one of the villains (!), and I just could not settle on who should tell this story. I knew what had happened in the world of the story and I knew what I wanted to say, but not how to say it. I felt like Austin Powers stuck sideways in that corridor on a cart, trying to adjust and adjust and adjust till I could move forward again. Finally, I realized that to get the tone I wanted, I would need *more* distance, not less—not a case of "We know what happened and here it is" but "We genuinely do not know what happened and that's scarier."

If readers looked at three stories in this book, what would you want them to be, and why?

I think I would pick "The General's Turn", "The Honeymakers", and "The Redoubtables"—not because (I am noticing) these are examples of good titles, yikes, but because I think it's kind of a representative range of the things I tend to be interested in. We go from war and mythology in a secondary-world setting, to folk horror with bees and gods, to weird science and a giant cover-up. I also think these three have some of the biggest unanswered questions and vaguest "What happens next" endings, which are my two favorite things in the world.

Is there anything else you'd like readers to know about this book?

Close readers of both the stories and the Beneath the Rising trilogy will probably spot a few somewhat intentional/somewhat unintentional Easter eggs! *Beneath* was on sub so long that between sending it out and having the book come out, it overlapped with a ton of stories being written and published. Also, as time went on and two more books appeared in the trilogy, there were callbacks from the novels to short stories as well. Sometimes it was because I wasn't paying attention (oops) but sometimes it's a deliberate reference.

Thinking on your larger body of work, are there stories that you were especially happy with, that you felt very strongly about, but that, for whatever reasons, just didn't get noticed the way other pieces did?

Definitely "These Lifeless Things", which was a sidequel (is that a word?) novella to a favorite short story of mine ("And Sneer of Cold Command", which was in my initial story collection submission but got bumped out of the table of contents because Michael thought it didn't fit in). I think "Lifeless" is one of the best, most heartfelt things I've ever written; I think it did exactly what I wanted it to in every respect. There's an amazing audio version with two different voice actors for the two first-person POV narrators in the story. It won a Subjective Chaos award. And it has sold practically zero copies and I don't think even my closest friends have read it. It just kinda never took off and I'm always quietly so sad about that—it was written in 2017 but I still keep thinking I could never write anything that strong now.

What else are you working on, what do you have coming up that you'd like readers to know about?

Stay tuned for sequels to *The Annual Migration of Clouds*, a novella from *Tordotcom* ("The Butcher of the Forest"), and a novel from Solaris (*The Siege of Burning Grass*, which I think wasn't announced? Or in the announcement it just said something like "Untitled Fantasy Novel") in the next couple of years!

I also have my first translated book coming out this summer with Editorial Cronos—they're translating *These Lifeless Things* and *And What Can We Offer You Tonight* into Catalan and publishing them as one book, which is super exciting! I should also have a handful of short stories coming out in various anthologies (*Life Beyond Us* with Laksa Publishing, *Robotic Ambitions* with Apex, *Wilted Pages* with Shortwave, *Reinvented Detective* with Pulse Publishing, and probably a couple others I'm forgetting). I also just had a story come out in *Small Wonders Magazine*, and in *The Other Side of Never*, which was a Peter Pan anthology edited by Paul Kane and Marie O'Regan for Titan.

ABOUT THE AUTHOR

Arley Sorg is co-Editor-in-Chief at *Fantasy Magazine* and a 2021 World Fantasy Award Finalist. He is also a finalist for two 2022 Ignyte Awards, for his work as a critic as well as for his creative nonfiction. Arley is senior editor at *Locus Magazine*, associate editor at both *Lightspeed* & *Nightmare*, and a columnist for *The Magazine of Fantasy and Science Fiction*. He takes on multiple roles, including slush reader, movie reviewer, and book reviewer, and conducts interviews for multiple venues, including *Clarkesworld Magazine* and his own site: arleysorg.com. He has taught classes and run workshops for Clarion West, *Augur Magazine*, and more, and has been a guest speaker at a range of events. Arley grew up in England, Hawaii, and Colorado, and studied Asian Religions at Pitzer College. He lives in the SF Bay Area and writes in local coffee shops when he can. Arley is a 2014 Odyssey Writing Workshop graduate.

Exploration And Healing: A Conversation with Megan O'Keefe

ARLEY SORG

Megan O'Keefe is from Seattle, and spent time on Whidbey Island, then later on the Oregon coast before moving to the San Francisco Bay Area. "I've enjoyed aspects of all of those places but cold, rocky beaches remain my favorite environments." She was "raised amongst journalists, and as soon as she was able joined them by crafting a newsletter which chronicled the daily adventures of the local cat population." Her first experiences with writing were for role-playing games, Dungeons & Dragons and White Wolf games in particular, for sessions with friends and in forums. In 2013 she started thinking about writing as a serious endeavor, with the *Writing Excuses* podcast as both inspiration and a source of craft information. In 2014, while still running her soap-making business, she sent the manuscript out which would quickly land her an agent and a book deal.

Before her debut novel hit the market, O'Keefe made her mark with short fiction, winning the fourth quarter section in the Writers of the Future contest with short story "Another Range of Mountains." Shortly after, in January 2015, O'Keefe's "Of Blood and Brine" appeared in *Shimmer Magazine*. Later that year the Barnes & Noble blog published her short story "The Fight Before Christmas."

In 2016 Angry Robot published O'Keefe's debut, *Steal the Sky*, about a con man and his best friend trying to steal an airship—of course, things don't go as planned. Originally drafted in about three weeks as a means to wind-down from writing a previous book, O'Keefe realized she had put together something remarkable, and revised it from roughly 70K words to about 117K words. *Steal the Sky* won a Morningstar Award and launched a series, continued with *Break the Chains, Inherit the Flame*, and *The Proposal Game*.

In 2019 Orbit published O'Keefe's first novel in a new series, an epic space opera called *Velocity Weapon*. The book was well received, earning praise from venues like *Locus* and *Publishers Weekly*, the latter of which described it as "a complicated, thoughtful tale that skillfully interweaves intrigue, action, and strong characterization." 2019 was also the year that O'Keefe went full-time writer. "Like many writers, I held a pretty eclectic mix of jobs before that. I've worked in graphic design, art curation, webdev, and in perfumery." Sequels *Chaos Vector* followed in 2020, and *Catalyst Gate* in 2021. Earlier that year, Orbit also released a hundred and four-page standalone *The First Omega* in digital format.

When she's not writing, Megan O'Keefe has "far too many hobbies to list," and says on her site that she "spends her free time tinkering with anything she can get her hands on." Over the years her most consistent hobbies have been programming and music, in particular metal, punk, and industrial. "I tend to go where the hyperfocus takes me . . . Recently I've been applying this primarily to gamedev, and have probably spent far too much time pondering state machine implementation. One day I'll title a story *Pushdown Automata*, I'm sure. I'm also sure marketing won't like that title and I'll have to change it, hah."

The Blighted Stars is due from Orbit later this month, beginning O'Keefe's brand new epic space opera trilogy called the Devoured Worlds. Book two, *The Fractured Dark*, is scheduled for September 2023.

Who were some of the most important writers for you when you started getting into genre fiction, what were some of the most important works? And do they still hold up?

The first fantasy book I picked up off the shelf on my own was *Ombria in Shadow* by Patricia A. McKillip. I devoured it, and then everything else she'd written. While I haven't revisited her works in ages, I'd be surprised if they didn't hold up. They are beautifully written, and I was originally drawn to them because the femme characters got to *do* things and be people, flaws and all, which was harder to find at the time.

My other first love of fantasy was Terry Pratchett. I actually began the Discworld books with *The Colour of Magic*, which I'm told is illegal, but Pratchett's scathing wit hooked me regardless. Anyone who claims his work doesn't hold up is welcome to fight me in a Denny's parking lot.

Do you see any of these writers in your own work, or do you have a different set of literary influences?

Absolutely. Everything we consume influences the art we make—that's what art is, really. Human synthesis of experience. Naturally my influences range wider—everything from stand-up comedy, to music, to video games, to a wide array of other literary works—but the things you imprint on when you're younger always stay with you.

Your upcoming book, The Blighted Stars, is described as the beginning of a new epic space opera trilogy. What is wonderful about Space Opera as a genre for you? What are the best things about it from a writer's perspective?

To me, Space Opera is fundamentally about exploration—literally and figuratively. I tend to think of it as a larger wrapper with the possibility of enfolding many other genres. A space opera can be horror, romance, a cozy, a mystery—anything at all, really—and those subgenres will always inherit the greater sense of exploration and wonder from Space Opera. As both a reader and writer, I find this variety a delight.

Before the publication of your debut novel, Steal the Sky, you had a few short stories come out, but it looks like your career has been more focused on books since then. Is short fiction no longer of interest, or are you secretly building up to launch a collection?

I've always been a long-from writer at heart. While I love reading short stories, it's rare I have an idea for one that isn't actually a novel pretending at being a short story. That said, I do have a few shorts lingering on the back burner that I'd like to finish editing, some day. Contracted work takes priority, though, and I'm very single-minded when I'm working on a story. My mind lives fully in that world, and I find it damages the work to switch gears back and forth.

In terms of process, when you are first drafting a novel, what do you focus on most?

Flow. While I write extensive outlines, I also draft very, very quickly. This is partly the result of hyperfocus and partly because it's something I've simply trained myself to do over the years. Getting the words down quickly helps me feel out how they all flow together—I save the granular edits for after my rough draft. If something feels jarring, if a scene doesn't want to be written, then there's usually something wrong with it and I need to go back to my outline to re-evaluate why that is.

Drafting, for me, is a very closed-door process where I'm primarily following how the text is making me feel as I write it. Am I bored? Is this dragging on too long? Do I feel like I missed something important? Am I anxious to skip this part to get to the "good bit"—and why? Are all questions at the forefront of my mind during the rough draft stage.

I've seen a number of reviews praising your work, including calling out your excellent worldbuilding. For you, in terms of craft, what is the key to great worldbuilding?

This is going to be a terribly annoying answer, because the only honest advice I have is that it depends entirely on the world you're trying to build. Stay true to the story you want to tell, and focus on the details that matter to support that story. It's tempting to say something prescriptive, like—if your story is character-driven, don't spend a whole page describing a piece of technology. But if that piece of tech matters to your character, then you absolutely should be focusing on how it works and what they think about it.

What was the initial inspiration for The Blighted Stars, and how did the book develop?

I keep a folder of ideas that capture my interest as they come to me. Dialogue lines, names, places, concepts, etc. *The Blighted Stars* began as a doc titled "Sixth Cradle" and all the doc has written in it is: "enemies to lovers, mycorrhizal, they're probably not even human anymore." I have no idea where that came from, but when it came time to pitch options to Orbit after *Catalyst Gate* I skimmed though my notes and that one stuck out to me.

I always write a synopsis first, as I find it gives me both a solid framework and something to reference when I get lost in the weeds on the nitty gritty of plot points. While building up the outline, I re-read John McPhee's *Annals of the Former World* and Merlin Sheldrake's *Entangled Life* to get the mood right. I've described *The Blighted Stars* as *Annals* and *Entangled* kiss under decaying mistletoe, and I stand by that comparison even if it's terribly niche, hah.

What were the most challenging things about writing this book, and getting the new series started?

Velocity Weapon is known for the plot twist at the central point of the story. I went into *The Blighted Stars* knowing that readers who followed me from The Protectorate trilogy would be on high-alert for similar narrative shenanigans. My goal, from the outset, was to leave breadcrumbs for those readers while still, I hope, managing to surprise them in a satisfying way.

What is the heart of The Blighted Stars for you, what do you want readers to know, beyond blurbs and reviews?

The Devoured Worlds trilogy was written as a whole unit over the course of 2020-2021. A few things happened, during that time frame. My tendency is to write fairly fast-paced stories; my drafts are always shorter than they need to be. But when I approached TDW I did so with the intention of making space for greater interiority. Of giving the characters the chance to process what's happened to them. Naira is forever under immense pressure, and one of the central conceits of the story's romance is that both protagonists allow each other the time to stop, and process, and maybe even heal. The time investment in reading a book, let alone a trilogy, can sometimes feel like a fantastical indulgence all on its own. I hope we can all allow ourselves, and each other, to indulge a little more in the things that help us heal. And I am deeply honored by any reader who chooses to spend that time with a story of my making.

What else are you working on, what do you have coming up that you'd like readers to know about?

The Devoured Worlds trilogy is on a quick release schedule, so book two, *The Fractured Dark*, will be out on September 26th of this year. I'm also returning to the sky pirate vibes of *Steal the Sky* in a standalone space opera that should be coming out sometime in the next year. It features sapphic space pirates, stained glass superstructures, and an unknown intelligence. It was a blast to write, and is actually the expanded version of my 2020 NaNoWriMo novel.

ABOUT THE AUTHOR

Arley Sorg is co-Editor-in-Chief at *Fantasy Magazine* and a 2021 World Fantasy Award Finalist. He is also a finalist for two 2022 Ignyte Awards, for his work as a critic as well as for his creative nonfiction. Arley is senior editor at *Locus Magazine*, associate editor at both *Lightspeed* & *Nightmare*, and a columnist for *The Magazine of Fantasy and Science Fiction*. He takes on multiple roles, including slush reader, movie reviewer, and book reviewer, and conducts interviews for multiple venues, including *Clarkesworld Magazine* and his own site: arleysorg.com. He has taught classes and run workshops for Clarion West, *Augur Magazine*, and more, and has been a guest speaker at a range of events. Arley grew up in England, Hawaii, and Colorado, and studied Asian Religions at Pitzer College. He lives in the SF Bay Area and writes in local coffee shops when he can. Arley is a 2014 Odyssey Writing Workshop graduate.

Editor's Desk: Something Went Mostly Right

NEIL CLARKE

I've spent the last two editorials focused on things that have caused major disruptions at *Clarkesworld*: a loss of revenue due to Amazon's discontinuation of its digital subscription program and how our open submissions process has been impacted by LLMs like ChatGPT. While both issues are ongoing and important, this month I want to change things up and spend some time talking about something that went mostly right.

I've long held that translation is an important, and often overlooked, element in what shapes the future of science fiction. Great stories can come from anyone, anywhere. It is not the sole domain of a region, people, or language.

In celebrating ten years of translation at *Clarkesworld*, I wrote in a 2021 editorial:

> "I am not the first editor to feel passionately about the importance of translated and international science fiction. Many editors before me have shared the sentiment, sometimes warning us of the hazards of isolation. One of my favorite quotes on this subject is by Lester Del Rey and was published in an editorial of *International Science-Fiction* in June 1968:
>
> ' . . . our stories are set to large numbers of fans and translators all over the world, while our own authors and fans seldom get even a hint of the work being done in our field by others. We're in serious danger of becoming the most provincial science-fiction readers—and writers—on earth.' "

Lester's warning went unheeded and for decades to follow, translated science fiction was difficult to find and almost exclusively on the fringes. Years passed without readers and writers benefiting from this important form of cross-pollination. While some progress has been made within the last decade, we've only just scratched the surface, with many doors still closed to writers working in other languages.

In November 2020, I acknowledged one significant way that we were contributing to that problem:

> "There's one point that I keep circling back around to as a problem and that's the 'English language only' in our submissions guidelines. As a monolingual editor with a limited budget, it's not shocking that this is present in our guidelines, but uncompromisingly expecting others to speak your language—or that they find someone to translate for them—isn't exactly compatible with our goals. It turns language into a barrier."

Practically speaking, there isn't a viable solution to this problem, at least nothing I can do on my own. I did, however, come up with a potentially-replicable model that would allow me, and perhaps others, to chip away at it. The original plan was to give it a trial run in 2021, but medical issues consumed a significant percentage of my time, leading to a work backlog that piled into 2022.

Finally, in early 2023, we were in a position to launch our pilot project. From January 15th through February 15th, we held our first open call for submissions written in Spanish, but never published in English.

The key element for this project was having a strong team that was well-aligned with our tastes and goals. I want to express my deepest gratitude to Nelly Geraldine Garcia-Rosas, Cristina Jurado, and Loreto ML for their time and work as part of the fiction team. They handled all of the first reading for the 1124 submissions we received, providing me with detailed summaries and personal assessments. From there, we narrowed the pile down to thirty-three works. Those endured a much more in-depth second round of consideration that ultimately led to the acceptance of eight stories that we will translate and publish over the course of next year.

In the interest of transparency, I want to explain how the second round evaluation process was carried out. Each of the thirty-three works was read by the entire team. In my case, that required the use of machine translation. These tools are horribly unreliable, but understanding that, I placed more emphasis on the reader's description and team members' individual feedback. Those bad translations often prompted me to ask more questions, which led to a better understanding of the strengths and weaknesses of each story. Just as with our English language submissions, there were strong works that were ultimately rejected because they didn't fit our publication. (If there was a trend among those, it might have been that they drifted a bit further into horror than I typically like.)

Overall, the volume of submissions, pass-up rate, and percentage of acceptances was in line with or slightly below an average month of English language submissions. The "slightly below" can probably be attributed to the volume of stories that rather deliberately ignored the science fiction focus of the call.

One of the other interesting observations was that in some regions, authors took our focused guidelines and "hard sell" list as telling them what they could or couldn't write, rather than what we would or wouldn't want to publish. There's reason to think that there may have involved cultural differences, a simple misunderstanding of the purpose of the call, or both. In our guidelines we made it clear that we weren't running a special issue. From the start, this was intended to place Spanish language science fiction alongside English language works as equals. Whatever the reason, however, our intent and reasons are something that we can communicate more clearly in future iterations.

Accepted stories were written by authors from Bolivia, Dominican Republic, Mexico, Spain, and Uruguay. Throughout the first couple of weeks of the call, I regularly posted social media updates indicating the number of submissions and where they were coming from. While there was a lot of interest in the data, it eventually began to play into some healthy and unhealthy regional competitiveness. While many authors were thrilled to see their country's numbers inching upwards, celebrating their colleagues' attempts, others were more focused on who had the most and behaving as if threatened by it. In turn, they spread disinformation about the project and sometimes made disparaging remarks about members of our team. Furthermore, after announcing our first acceptance, there were unfounded theories that we were showing favoritism to Spanish authors. (Spain was responsible for approximately half of the submissions at the time.) Others shared with us that this sort of regional competitiveness was not unusual. In the future, we'll step away from these regional politics by holding multiple regional calls rather than one entire-language call.

Shifting to smaller, regional calls will help us in another way as well. We were initially uncertain about the number of submissions we would receive and guessed too low. For the volume of submissions received, we should have had a team twice as large. While our initial fiction team included five people, there was some attrition during training. At the time, the losses were considered within our margin of safety. Having gone through this once, a bigger team would have sped things up, but might have over-complicated matters in round two. Regional calls should have the side-effect of maintaining a more healthy submissions volume and allow us to swap replacement team members in and out more easily.

Beyond that, deciding to publicly announce the first sale while the window was still open turned out to be a mistake. When it was discovered that the author's story had AI and humor elements, we saw a dramatic shift in the volume of humorous or AI-related stories in our queue. While we have nearly seventeen years of stories on our site, many of the authors took their guidance from that one acceptance. It suggests that many of the authors participating were previously unfamiliar with our work, which would have been anticipated if we had actually stopped to think about it. In our enthusiasm to celebrate our first acceptance, we tainted the pool. That mistake won't happen again.

So, overall, things went mostly right. We managed to find eight stories—several by authors who haven't been published in English before—and give the tires on this new submission model a good kick. I'm in the process of commissioning the translations for these stories and then I'll move onto making some software updates for next time.

And yes, there will be a next time. With everything else that is going on, that might take some time, but we will get there!

ABOUT THE AUTHOR

Neil Clarke is the editor of *Clarkesworld Magazine, Forever Magazine,* and several anthologies, including the Best Science Fiction of the Year series. He is a ten-time finalist and current winner of the Hugo Award for Best Editor (Short Form), has won the Chesley Award for Best Art Director three times, and received the Kate Wilhelm Solstice Award from SFWA in 2019. His latest anthology, *New Voices in Chinese Science Fiction* (co-edited with Xia Jia and Regina Kanyu Wang), is now available from Clarkesworld Books. He currently lives in NJ with his wife and two sons.

Taking a Sample

COVER ART BY ARTHUR HAAS

ABOUT THE ARTIST

Arthur Haas is a concept artist from Amsterdam, the Netherlands. He specializes in environment design and concept art for the entertainment industry and has a passion for science fiction. Arthur works as a freelance artist for major Hollywood film studios and international book publishers, and sells original artworks online and in galleries.

Manufactured by Amazon.ca
Acheson, AB

11043919R00090